Paralyzed

Jeff Rud

orca sports

Orca Book Publishers

Library and Archives Canada Cataloguing in Publication

Rud, Jeff, 1960-
Paralyzed / written by Jeff Rud.

(Orca sports)
ISBN 978-1-55469-059-6

I. Title. II. Series.

PS8635.U32P37 2008   jC813'.6   C2008-903053-2

Summary: A football tackle gone wrong puts a boy
in hospital and leaves star linebacker Reggie Scott
feeling confused, guilty and alone.

First published in the United States, 2008
Library of Congress Control Number: 2008928571

Orca Book Publishers gratefully acknowledges the support for its publishing
programs provided by the following agencies: the Government of Canada
through the Book Publishing Industry Development Program and the
Canada Council for the Arts, and the Province of British Columbia through
the BC Arts Council and the Book Publishing Tax Credit.

Cover design by Bruce Collins
Cover photography by Materfile
Author photo by Deborah McCarron

Orca Book Publishers
PO Box 5626, Stn. B
Victoria, BC Canada
V8R 6S4

Orca Book Publishers
PO Box 468
Custer, WA USA
98240-0468

www.orcabook.com
Printed and bound in Canada.
Printed on 100% PCW recycled paper.
11 10 09 08 • 4 3 2 1

For Becky, a terrific niece

Acknowledgments

Thanks to both Bob Tyrrell and Andrew Wooldridge of Orca Book Publishers for their continued strong support. Thanks also to editor Sarah Harvey, who did her usual tremendous job in steering this project to completion. Finally, thanks to my wife, Lana, and our children, Maggie and Matt, for all you do.

chapter one

Keith Hobart's eyes were a dead giveaway. The Milbury quarterback's right arm and body told me he was throwing a swing pass to the big fullback who was cutting briskly to my left. But Hobart's eyes said otherwise. For just a split second, they flickered to the right and that was enough. My instincts took over.

They didn't let me down. I jammed my left foot into the turf and lunged the opposite way. I was just in time to see the football heading toward the tight end, all alone in the flats about ten yards deep. If he caught the ball, he was going a long way. *If* he caught the ball, that is. That wasn't going to happen.

I leaped, stabbing out my right hand and batting the football from the air. It fell into my left arm, and I slapped both hands over it. Interception! Plays like this were what every high school middle linebacker lived for.

My eyes darted downfield, scanning the best route. There were more of my team's black jerseys to my left. I cut sharply that way. If I could just get outside...

"Ughhh!" I heard myself groan. I felt the air rudely pushed from my lungs before I realized what was happening. I hadn't even heard Nate Brown's cleats thundering behind me. But I certainly heard the thud of his helmet hitting my backside. And felt it. My legs caved underneath me, and I dropped to the ground. *Hold on to the ball! Hold on to it!*

Even as I hit the turf hard, I managed to keep the football tightly gripped in my hands. I immediately jumped up, holding it above my head in triumph. I looked over at our bench, where Coach Clark and the offensive team were celebrating. I glanced the other way and saw Keith Hobart, the Milbury quarterback, walking dejectedly off the field. It was only the first quarter of the first game of my senior season at Lincoln. I already had a pickoff. I was pumped.

"Lincoln interception by number seventy-seven, Reggie Scott." The announcer's voice rang across the stadium, validating my big play.

My celebration was short-lived. As I continued to dance around with the ball in my outstretched arms, I sensed a commotion on the field a few feet behind me. I glanced back. Nate Brown, the Milbury tight end, was still lying on the ground. Something wasn't right.

The game officials surrounded him. They motioned to the Milbury sidelines for help from the training staff. The expressions on their faces told me that football, at this moment, was the furthest thing from their minds.

The referee motioned for us to return to our benches. From the sidelines, I looked out to midfield where Brown still lay. He was surrounded by Milbury coaches and training staff. Dr. Stevens, who was on-call for all our Lincoln home games, was out there too.

"What's wrong with him?" I asked. Nobody on the sidelines answered. Coach Clark huddled our offense together. They were going over their plays for the next series. Coach Molloy, our defensive coordinator, patted me on the back. "Nice hands, Reggie," he said. "Real nice hands."

I smiled at Coach Molloy. He and I got along well. He had taught me how to tackle as a middle schooler. I had managed to become one of the city's best middle linebackers in large part because of him. To hear his praise in our first game of the most important season of my life felt great.

Something wasn't right, though. Nate Brown was still lying out in the middle of the field. Dr. Stevens was kneeling beside him now, watching him intently and checking his pulse. My chest began to tighten, and I started to sweat. Why wasn't Nate getting up?

Then I heard the sirens, getting louder as they approached the Lincoln High School stadium. The ambulance didn't stop in the parking lot. The coaches had already opened the gate to the track that circled the football field. The ambulance pulled right onto the track and drove parallel to where the Milbury tight end lay. Still motionless.

As the siren shut off, I heard murmuring in the stands. By now everybody, including all the kids on our team, could sense there was something seriously wrong. The coaches stopped talking to the players. Everybody stopped thinking about the game. All of us were fixated on Nate Brown.

The paramedics brought a stretcher with them as they crossed the field. They had another device I recognized from TV medical shows. It was a "halo" used to keep an accident victim's neck stable in the case of a spinal injury.

The paramedics took their time. They talked to the coaches and the doctor; they took Nate's pulse and examined him carefully. They fitted the halo around his neck and head and gingerly lifted him onto the stretcher. This was no ordinary football injury.

A middle-aged couple had rushed down from the stands to the boy's side. They must be Nate Brown's parents. They were talking to the coaches and the paramedics. The woman, a tall redhead dressed in a Milbury hoodie and jeans, collapsed onto her knees, sobbing. The man just stood there, staring down at his son.

The paramedics slowly removed Nate from the field on the stretcher. A kid on the Milbury sidelines began clapping, something we always did when a player got up after being injured. But Nate hadn't gotten up. Still, we followed his lead, applauding too. So did the folks in the stands. What else were we supposed to do?

The coaches huddled at midfield with the officials. They all nodded in agreement. Coach Clark, his face pale and his lips pursed, returned to our side of the field. "Let's go, guys," he said. "There isn't going to be any more football today."

I was stunned. A few minutes earlier, we had all been full of adrenaline and emotion. Now we were silently trudging back to our locker room. This was worse than a loss. A lot worse.

Coach Clark's gray eyes met mine. "Reggie," he said softly, "come here a minute."

Everybody else was filing quietly into the locker room. Coach pulled me behind the door, out of sight of my teammates. "I just want to be sure you know that this wasn't your fault," he said. "You know that, right, Reggie?"

"Uh, yeah, sure," I said. I hadn't really thought about it being anybody's fault until now. "What's wrong with him, Coach? Is he going to be all right?"

Coach Clark shook his head slowly. "I don't know," he said. "I'd like to tell you he's going to be fine, but he wasn't moving. The paramedics are worried about paralysis."

I gulped. *Paralysis.* "But he'll be fine, right?" I said. "I mean, they'll fix him at the hospital."

The coach just stared down at the ground. "I can't tell you anything more than that, Reggie," he said. "But I can tell you again that it definitely wasn't your fault. The boy hit you. He had his helmet down. I've told all you kids for as long as I can remember that it's dangerous to hit like that. Now you know why."

I nodded. One of the first things my tackle football coaches had taught me in Pop Warner was never to lead with your helmet. It was illegal. They called it spearing. Still, I had seen plenty of kids do it over the years. But nobody had ever been paralyzed before.

Coach and I walked into the locker room. The players were changing quietly and grumbling about the game being cancelled. I wasn't thinking much about the game. It didn't seem very important now.

chapter two

I was in a daze, changing out of my football gear in silence. I didn't feel much like talking. It was weird. I had felt him hit me, and everything had just seemed normal. Like a thousand other football plays I had been part of.

"Hey, Reggie." Jeff Stevens's deep voice snapped me out of my thoughts. Jeff was Dr. Stevens's son and our wide receiver. "Feel like coming over tonight to play some

Xbox 360? I got the new *Madden* game this week."

Jeff was one of my best friends. Normally, I would have loved nothing better than to spend Friday night at his place. The Stevens family lived in a huge house in the ritzy Camelot neighborhood, not far north of Lincoln High. They had a big swimming pool and a hot tub. Jeff's mom was a terrific cook. But I just didn't feel like it tonight.

"I can't. Plans with my family." I wasn't really lying, but I wasn't exactly telling the truth, either. My parents were at the game. I was riding home with them, but we didn't have anything special planned.

"Okay. See you at practice tomorrow," Jeff said. At the Saturday sessions, our team usually reviewed video of the previous night's game and then ran through a light, no-pads workout. There wouldn't be much video to watch tomorrow, though.

"Later," I said, watching Jeff leave the locker room. I wasn't far behind him. I just wanted to get out of the stadium and think about something other than football.

Mom and Dad were just outside the locker room door. I guess I had taken longer than usual to get changed. There were only a few other sets of parents still waiting.

"Hey, kiddo!" Dad said with a grin. "How are you doing?"

"I'm okay," I said. "I mean, it was kind of weird with them stopping the game. I hope Nate's all right."

"Me too," said Mom, her eyes opening wide. "The first thing that came to my mind when I saw that boy lying there on the field was that it could have been you. I don't even want to think about it..."

Mom put her hand up to her mouth and drew a deep breath.

"Well, it wasn't me," I said.

"Do you know the kid?" Dad asked. "I didn't recognize the number."

I nodded. "It's Nate Brown. I've been at a couple of football camps with him.

He's a nice guy. A good tight end too. He's really quick."

Nobody said anything. I could tell we were all thinking the same thing: We hoped Nate Brown would still be quick after today.

We walked out to the parking lot. I was just buckling up in the backseat of the Bronco when Mom said, "We thought we'd take you out for a victory supper tonight. You guys didn't get to play the whole game, but we'll still go out. What do you feel like?"

I mulled it over for a few seconds. I wasn't really feeling hungry. In fact, my mind was not on food at all. It was on Nate Brown. I kept seeing him being carried off the field. I kept seeing his mother breaking down on the field.

"Can we go to the hospital?" I said it so fast I surprised even myself. "I'm kind of worried about Nate. I mean, he wasn't even moving."

Dad had already left the stadium parking lot. As I spoke, he pulled the car over and stopped.

"Reggie," he said, turning his head and looking directly into my eyes. Mom was staring at me too. "It was an accident. What happened to that boy wasn't your fault."

I knew it wasn't my fault. Why did everybody feel like they had to tell me that?

"I know," I said. "I just want to make sure he's okay."

"I'll tell you what," Dad replied gently. "We'll go out and grab a bite to eat. Then we'll go home and maybe watch a movie. You can go check on Nate at the hospital tomorrow after practice."

I nodded.

"Maybe he'll even be out by then," Mom said.

I didn't say anything. But somehow, I doubted that very much.

We went to Sperlini's for pasta. Normally, I would have been happy to get a big plate of tortellini with meat sauce, a Caesar salad and a Coke. But I still wasn't hungry. I asked the waiter for a half-order and a water.

"You feeling okay?" Mom said. "Usually you're hungrier than this after a game."

"We didn't exactly get a full game in, Mom," I replied. That got me thinking about Nate Brown all over again. As Mom and Dad talked, I stared ahead at the big-screen television on the wall. It was playing a European soccer game. I tuned everything out. My mind was somewhere else.

chapter three

I woke up early the next morning to the sound of geese honking. I got up and went to my window and watched intently as an entire flock flapped past our house. They were flying unusually low, in a V, with one bird leading the way. The rest of them followed the leader, in nearly perfect formation.

I knew these geese were going south for the winter. Pretty much every fall,

I saw the same thing: These huge beautiful birds flying together, honking noisily. Dad had told me about how geese take turns at being the leader. I thought it was pretty cool that these birds were smart enough to share the responsibility. None of them got too tired.

I had only been thinking about the geese for a few seconds when thoughts of Nate Brown rushed back into my head. I felt butterflies in the pit of my stomach. I wondered how he was doing and whether he was out of hospital yet.

Mom and Dad were already up and eating breakfast. Dad had the Saturday *Times* spread across the kitchen island, as usual. Mom was reading a novel. Saturday morning was pretty relaxed around our house. I didn't feel relaxed this morning.

"Hey, kiddo," Dad said. "Have a good sleep?"

I nodded. But I got right to the point. "Can we go to the hospital today?" I said. "I really want to see if Nate is okay."

Mom looked concerned. She glanced at Dad and then fixed her blue eyes on me. "You have something to eat and go to practice, and then I'll take you up there," she said.

Dad was reading the front section of the newspaper. I snatched the sports section of the *Times* from the pile under him. It was our usual routine on Saturday. It was the only section of the paper I ever read.

I flipped past the college football coverage and checked out the prep scores from last night. Although we hadn't got to finish our game, there had been plenty of other high school action. I was curious to see how all the other teams in the city had done in their season-openers.

The headline running across the top of the inside page caught my eye immediately. *Milbury star suffers serious injury.* Once again, I felt queasy. But now it was much worse than before.

Promising Milbury High School tight end Nate Brown remained in hospital last night after being injured in a game at Lincoln High, the story began.

Brown, a six-foot senior, was hurt as he attempted to tackle Lincoln's Reggie Scott early in the first quarter. Brown was removed from the field on a stretcher and taken to Gower General Hospital.

Medical staff at Gower would not provide any information on Brown's condition last night. But the injury was considered serious enough that the season-opening game between Milbury and Lincoln was halted.

I scanned the article to the bottom, looking for more information on Nate. But there was none. Obviously, though, the injury was serious if the newspaper was doing a separate story on it.

"Did you see this?" I asked my parents, my voice croaking. "I wish it said how he was doing."

"Don't worry, Reggie," Dad said. "There's nothing you can do about it anyway. You get ready for practice. Mom will take you up there afterward."

I went upstairs to wash my face and brush my teeth. About the last thing I felt like doing this morning was playing football. But maybe somebody there would know something more about Nate's condition.

Dad drove me to Lincoln, mostly in silence. He could tell I was stewing about Nate Brown. There wasn't much he could say to make me feel better.

I got out and began heading to the gym. Dad pulled alongside me and rolled down his window partway.

"Reggie," he said, "you can't dwell on this. Just try to forget about it. Go out there and have some fun."

"Okay, Dad," I replied. But I didn't feel okay, and I certainly wasn't going to be able to forget about it. What if Nate never walked again?

I seemed to be the only one preoccupied with Nate Brown. The accident the night before was only mentioned once—as we watched the brief videotape of the first quarter.

Just a few plays in, the sequence that caused the injury flickered across the big-screen TV at the front of the room. There was me making the right read and picking off the football. There was me looking upfield. Then, suddenly, there was Nate Brown, lowering his head and slamming into my backside with his helmet.

I could see now that Brown's head had collided directly with my hip. He had fallen straight to the ground. As my teammates cheered my interception on the screen, I could only watch Brown lying there, motionless.

"I wanted you guys to see this," Coach Clark said, striding to the front of the room. "Smitty, can you get the lights?"

Travis Smith, our manager, flicked on the lights and turned off the TV. Coach Clark continued.

"What happened to that boy was very unfortunate," he said. "But it was entirely preventable. It was caused completely—one hundred percent—by poor tackling technique. Not just poor, but sloppy and dangerous.

"Nobody should ever lead with their helmet. It is not a weapon, gentlemen. It is for protection. When somebody tackles like this boy did last night, it can result in a serious injury."

Pete Fulton blurted out what everybody in the room was thinking. Or certainly what was on my mind. "Is he okay?"

"We don't know," Coach Clark said. "We haven't got an update yet. But as soon as we have one, we'll let you know."

The practice that followed was the usual Saturday morning drill. No pads, no hitting. Just a lot of sprints, some light passing and coverage practice. The coach blew his whistle whenever somebody was out of position.

Still, it dragged for me. My head wasn't into football. All I could think about was Nate Brown lying there. The rest of us were able to run and laugh and joke this morning, but what about him?

When practice finished, I dressed quickly, not bothering to shower since we hadn't worked hard enough to sweat much. I grabbed a couple of textbooks out of my locker and headed out to the parking lot to wait for Mom.

A few minutes later, she pulled up in the minivan. The back was full of groceries. Mom's usual Saturday fall routine was to do the shopping and then pick me up from our workout.

"Well," she said as I climbed in, "how was practice?"

"Okay, I guess," I said. "We didn't do much. Saturday's usually pretty light."

"I picked up some of that corned beef you like and some nice rye bread," Mom said. "Thought we'd have it for lunch on the patio and then—"

"What about the hospital?" I said. "I thought we were going there to check on Nate."

"Well, I've got this van full of groceries," Mom said. "I've got ice cream and meat in here that probably won't keep in this sun."

"Can you drop me off there, then?" I said. "I can get home on my own."

Mom looked worried. "Reggie, let's just go home. I can take you to the hospital later if you still want to go. But come home and have some lunch first."

"I'm not hungry," I said curtly. "Just drop me off at the hospital, okay?"

I immediately regretted the tone in my voice. But I was getting irritated. Why didn't my parents want me to go to the hospital?

"All right," Mom said. "I can come back and pick you up later."

"It's okay. I'll catch a bus."

Mom turned down Commercial, away from home and in the direction of Gower General. She asked me a few questions about football and school along the way. All I could manage were one-word answers. I was obsessed with getting to the hospital and making sure Nate was okay.

Once we were in the hospital parking lot, I jumped out of the van and headed up the steps to the main entrance. I had been inside Gower General only once before—the time I had broken my leg falling off my bike when I was six. Hospitals still scared me.

The main lobby was crowded. Doctors and nurses, patients and family members milled about. I spotted the reception desk and waited in line to ask where to find Nate.

"Can I help you?" said the woman behind the desk. She was about the only staff member not wearing a white coat or a set of green hospital scrubs.

"Can you tell me how to get to Nate Brown's room?" I asked.

The woman looked at her screen and typed Nate's name into her computer. "Nathaniel Brown," she said after a few seconds. "He's still in ICU, room three-one-six. Are you family?"

I shook my head. "What's ICU?"

"That's the Intensive Care Unit. It's on the third floor. But he can't have visitors unless you're family."

"But I have to see him," I said. "I need to see if he's all right."

The receptionist's face softened. She could sense that I was desperate. "I'll tell you what," she said. "Take that elevator up to the third floor and speak to the head nurse at the ICU station. That's the best I can do."

I nodded and thanked her. I pressed the UP button and waited for the elevator. When the door opened, I was staring at a tall orderly in green scrubs. He was standing beside a gurney. On the gurney was a patient with tubes sticking out of his nose, mouth and arm. "Come on in," the orderly said.

There wasn't much room in the elevator, but I squeezed in beside the gurney. The sick man was asleep, and I didn't say anything to the orderly. I got out of the elevator on the third floor, relieved to get away from the man on the gurney. Hospitals creeped me out. I hadn't been around much serious illness. It wasn't something I knew about or felt comfortable with. I preferred to keep it that way.

I found the head nurse's station and, again, waited my turn.

"What can I help you with?" The head nurse had jet-black hair, a thin face and friendly hazel eyes.

"I came to see Nate Brown, er, Nathaniel Brown," I replied.

"I'm sorry, but he can't have any visitors," she said gently. "Are you a family member?"

I shook my head. "I'm a friend. Sort of. I was playing football against him last night when he got hurt."

"It's a real shame," the nurse said. "So young..."

"Can you at least tell me how he's doing?" I knew I sounded desperate, but I needed to know right now that Nate was going to be okay.

"Let me check with somebody. Maybe I can get you an update," she said as she turned and walked quickly down the hall and around the corner.

In a few minutes, she returned. Alongside her was the tall redheaded woman that I had seen last night on the football field. The one who had been sobbing beside Nate Brown.

The woman was staring at me intently. She looked confused.

"I don't know you," she said loudly as she and the nurse approached us. "Are you a teammate of Nate's?"

"No," I said solemnly. "I play for Lincoln. It was me with him on that play..."

The woman's face changed in an instant. Gone was the mournful, confused look. In its place was a flash of anger. Her face grew red, and her eyelids twitched.

"What are you doing here?" she said harshly. "Why did you come?"

"I came to see Nate," I stammered. "To see if he's okay. I—"

"How do you think he's doing?" The woman was shrieking now. "This is the Intensive Care Unit. How the hell do you think he's doing?"

I didn't know what to say. "Maybe I should come back some other time." It was all I could think of.

"No, no...No!" she said. "Don't come back. Ever! I don't want you here. Nate doesn't want you here. I saw you dancing around after that play. I saw you celebrating. Don't think I didn't notice."

Her words hit me like a speeding train. Everybody had been telling me the accident wasn't my fault. Now Nate's mom was blaming me. My legs felt weak. I could hardly breathe.

"But it was an—" She didn't let me finish.

"Get out of here! Now!" she screamed. The nurse with the black hair wrapped her arms around Nate's mom, attempting to calm her down. She managed to turn her around and head her away from me.

"You'd better go," the nurse said to me over her shoulder. "Just go."

I turned and walked out of the ICU and into the third-floor lobby. Never had waiting for an elevator taken so long. Tears were streaming down my face, and my chest was heaving.

chapter four

I hurried through the crowded main lobby of the hospital, suddenly feeling like an intruder. I was still crying, but I lowered my head so that nobody would notice.

Outside, I waited by the bus stop. I knew which route to take to get home but now I wished I had let Mom pick me up. I needed to talk to her, to somebody.

As the bus rumbled down Commercial toward my neighborhood, I thought about what had occurred in the ICU ward. It seemed like a bad dream. Had Nate Brown's mother really screamed at me and told me to get out of the hospital?

Her words had hurt. Although everybody else had reassured me that what had happened to Nate wasn't my fault, I was suddenly convinced she was right. I mean, it was me who had collided with Nate. Had it been something I had done that had left him lying in a hospital bed? Did he have tubes sticking out of him like the man I had seen in the elevator? Had I somehow turned my hip into his head?

And what was it that his mom had said? That I had danced around after Nate got hurt? That's probably what it had looked like to her. But I had only been celebrating the interception. I hadn't known Nate was injured. I wouldn't have danced around if I had known.

An urge to study the video of the hit came over me. I had to see whether there was something I could have done—or not done—that would have protected Nate. I made a quick decision and got out at the next stop.

It was only a couple of blocks back to the corner of Ambassador and Commercial. From there, it was a ten-minute walk to Lincoln High. If my hunch was right, Coach Clark would still be there.

The coach's office was located right beside the locker room, at the far end of the Lincoln gym. I was relieved to see through the window that he was sitting at his desk, going over playbooks.

I knocked on the door. Coach Clark looked up, surprised to see me. "Hey, Reggie," he said. "Come on in. Sit down."

I pulled up the chair across from the coach's desk. Now I was nervous. I wasn't exactly sure why.

"What's up?" he said.

"I need to ask you a favor. I was wondering if I could borrow the video from last night's game."

Coach Clark wrinkled his forehead and squinted. "Why would you want that? There's barely any game to look at."

"I need it. To take another look..." The words caught in the back of my throat and I couldn't finish my sentence.

"I think I know what this is all about," Coach Clark said. "But I'm not going to give you that tape, Reggie."

"Why not?"

"Because there's nothing to see on it. Nate Brown hit you with his helmet. It was a dangerous hit. It wouldn't have mattered who he ran into. He might as well have been hitting a side of beef."

I nodded. Inside, I wasn't so sure I agreed.

"But I think it might make me feel better about it," I pleaded. "I mean, if I looked at it again, I could be sure."

"Or you could stare at it all night and see things that just aren't there," the coach countered. "Sorry, Reggie. But that's not healthy."

"I went to see him today," I said.

"You mean Nate Brown?"

"Yeah. But I couldn't...I wasn't family so they wouldn't let me in."

"That's pretty standard," Coach said. "In a few days, maybe you and the other co-captains will be able to go in and visit."

Again, I nodded. I didn't tell the coach about my run-in with Nate's mother. I was ashamed of it. I had done something to upset somebody whose world was already crashing down around her.

"I guess I'll see you later then," I said to the coach.

"Okay, Reggie," he replied. "Listen, try to enjoy the rest of the weekend. Don't let this bother you. I've already told you this, but I'll tell you again: It wasn't your fault."

Once again, those four words. The way coach said them made it seem so simple.

By the time I got home, it was nearly 5:00 PM. The sun was beginning to set behind the houses on our street. Mom and Dad were in the kitchen. Mom was standing by the stove, watching over a stir-fry. Dad was making a salad.

"Reggie," Mom said. "We were starting to get worried about you. How did it go at the hospital?"

"Not great," I said, slumping into a chair beside Dad. "Horrible, in fact."

Mom turned down the stove. Dad put down his knife. "How is Nate?" Mom said.

"I don't really know," I replied. I could feel the tears rising again. "They wouldn't let me see him. I'm not family."

"Don't take it personally, Reggie," Dad said. "I think that's pretty standard for the hospital."

I was sobbing now. Mom and Dad looked at each other, bewildered. "Reggie, what's wrong?" Mom said, putting her hand on my shoulder.

"Nate's mom," I said. "She yelled at me. She kicked me out of the hospital. It was messed up."

Dad looked at Mom. "I knew we should have gone in with him," he said. "Tell us exactly what happened, Reggie."

In a couple of emotional minutes, I spilled it all. How Mrs. Brown wouldn't listen to why I was there. How she accused me of hurting her son and of celebrating afterward.

Mom and Dad were both quiet for several seconds. Finally Mom spoke. "I'm sorry that happened," she said. "You didn't deserve that. Reggie, sometimes stress does strange things to people. If it was you lying there in a hospital bed, I'm not sure I would be acting rationally, either. I'm sure when things settle down she'll feel differently."

I wasn't so sure. I had seen the hatred in her eyes. I had felt the sting of her accusations. I had never felt so loathed.

"I'm going to bed," I said.

"Bed?" Dad said. "Supper's in a couple of minutes."

"I'm not really hungry," I said. "And it's been a crappy day."

I climbed the stairs to my room, closed the door behind me and flopped down on my bed. Outside, another group of geese honked their way past our house. I was too tired to get up and check them out.

chapter five

Nothing that happened on Sunday made me feel much better than I had the day before. I was still stinging from my experience with Mrs. Brown. I was still really worried about Nate's condition. What if he never walked again?

I woke up early Monday morning with a good idea. I could ask Jeff's dad if he knew how Nate was doing. I knew he sometimes worked on call at Gower General. He'd probably already checked up on Nate.

I tracked down Jeff at lunchtime. He was in the cafeteria, about to launch himself into a huge piece of pepperoni pizza.

"Yeah, I can ask him," Jeff said after I'd put the suggestion to him. "But why don't you come over after practice and ask him yourself? You can stay for supper."

It sounded like a good idea to me. I'd forgotten all about practice until Jeff reminded me. In fact, I realized that I hadn't thought too much about football all weekend.

Unlike Saturday's light session, we wore full gear for our Monday afternoon practice. As I pulled on my pads, I realized it was the first time I had geared up since the incident with Nate Brown.

For the first half hour, we did calisthenics and conditioning drills. Then everybody on the team ran through receiving and defensive coverage drills to warm up the quarterbacks' arms. I made a couple of nice shoestring catches off throws by Lance Turner, a co-captain with me and our starting quarterback. "You got some hands, boy," Turner joked. "We have to get you playing on the right side of the ball."

Once the preliminaries were out of the way, Coach Molloy took the defense to one side of the field. Coach Clark gathered the offensive players on the other.

"We're going to run live plays now, boys," Coach Clark said. "We didn't get to hit or block much on Friday, so we'll work on some of that today to make up for it. Hit hard and clean, just like it was a game."

Normally, I loved anything in practice that simulated real game action—especially when the linebackers got a chance to hit. All of us who played defense felt that our Lincoln receivers and running backs were a pretty cocky bunch. This was a rare opportunity to bring them down a notch or two.

But by now I was already counting the minutes until this practice would be over.

I was waiting for the chance to ask Dr. Stevens if Nate Brown was doing any better.

I did my best to concentrate on each play, though. Coach Molloy had no patience for guys who didn't pay attention or give a full effort. Three plays in, I saw Dexter Bart, our starting fullback, bursting through the middle of our defensive line. I drew a bead on him and prepared to bring him down with a tackle.

It should have been a routine play. But something happened. Not physically, but mentally. I moved in to tackle Bart, but for some reason, I couldn't do it. My legs suddenly went weak. I lunged at him and missed badly. Dexter easily sidestepped me and carried on down the field.

I heard the shrill whistle. I knew it was Coach Molloy. "Just what the heck was that exactly?" he yelled at me. "Reggie, I've seen better tackle attempts from the junior girls' volleyball team."

My ears burned, but I knew I deserved the criticism. I didn't understand why, but at the last second, I hadn't been able to hit Dexter.

As practice continued, I managed to at least make contact with the next few ball carriers that ventured into my zone. But I wasn't tackling with anywhere near my normal power. "Didn't you get enough food today, Reggie?" Coach Molloy said. "Better eat your Wheaties tomorrow, son. We got Franklin this Friday. Those boys can run."

Coach Molloy was referring to the Franklin Demons, one of the better teams in the city prep league. Franklin was always one of the toughest games on Lincoln's schedule. We'd have to be in top form to beat them. Right now, I didn't feel anywhere near top form.

"Sorry," I replied to Coach Molloy. "I just don't have any energy today. Maybe I've got the flu."

I was lying. There was nothing wrong with my energy level. I just didn't feel like hitting anybody. Not after what had happened to Nate Brown.

I kept it to myself. I didn't want to say anything to the coaches about how I was feeling. Middle linebackers were supposed to hit, and hit hard. If I didn't do that, I knew I wouldn't be starting for the Lincoln Lions for long.

"You still coming over?" Jeff Stevens called to me across the crowded smelly locker room.

"Yeah, sure," I replied.

We walked together toward Jeff's house.

"Coach says we'll be making up that game against Milbury sometime this season," Jeff said as we walked along.

"Yeah," I replied.

"I think we would have won it Friday if we'd finished."

"Probably," I said.

Jeff shook his head in exasperation. "What's wrong with you, dude?" he said. "You barely hit anybody in practice today, and now all I get is one-word answers. What's up?"

"I don't know," I said. "I guess the thing with Nate has me freaked out."

"Why?" Jeff said, shaking his head again. "It was the kid's own fault, just like Coach said. You didn't have anything to do with it, except that you were there."

"If I tell you something, can you keep it to yourself?" I asked.

Jeff nodded. I lowered my voice even though nobody else was around. I told him about going to the hospital the day before and about how Nate's mom had gone ballistic on me.

"That's harsh," Jeff said, his eyes widening. "But she probably didn't mean it. She must be pretty messed up right now."

We had reached Jeff's house, a sprawling, white, two-story home set back on about an acre of property. When I came here, I always felt as though I was visiting the White House. Jeff's house was so much bigger and more impressive than ours.

As usual, Jeff and I went around the side of the house and into the backyard. The kidney-shaped swimming pool sparkled in the late afternoon sun. Jeff's mom was lying in a recliner near the far end of the pool, reading a book. She waved us over.

"Reggie came over to talk to Dad," Jeff said. "Can he stay for supper?"

"Sure," replied his Mom. "We're having hamburgers, as soon as I fire up the barbecue."

"We can do that," Jeff said.

Jeff and I pulled the cover off the barbecue. Within a few seconds, he had it lit and warming up. When it was hot enough, his mom tossed on six burgers—two each for me and Jeff. In a few minutes, the aroma coming off the grill was heavenly.

"Smells great," Dr. Stevens said as he entered the backyard. "Hey, Reggie. How are you doing?"

"I'm okay," I lied. "I came over today to talk to you about something, though."

I was sure Dr. Stevens could sense the urgency in my voice. "Sure, Reggie. No problem. Let's sit down."

Jeff had gone inside, and his mom was tending to the barbecue. "So, what is it?" Dr. Stevens said. "Got an injury you want to talk about?"

"No," I replied. "It's not about me. It's about Nate Brown, the kid who got hurt Friday night. I was wondering if you knew how he was doing."

Dr. Stevens's broad face grew more serious. His eyes narrowed beneath bushy gray-flecked brows. "I was in to see him this morning, as a matter of fact," he said. "What can I tell you?"

"He's still in the hospital, then?" I said. I had secretly hoped that Nate had been released. Part of me had even been wishfully thinking that he might be back at football practice with Milbury today.

"I'm afraid so," Dr. Stevens said. "It looks like he's going to be in Gower for a while yet."

I gulped. We had been beating around the bush. It was time to ask the question I had been wondering all weekend.

"What's wrong with him? I mean, is he going to be okay eventually?"

"Well, Reggie, it's a little too early to tell," Dr. Stevens said. "He has swelling on his spinal column as a result of the collision. Sometimes when that happens, it can cause paralysis. That's what Nate has now. He has no movement or feeling from his waist down."

I was stunned. I looked out across the beautiful swimming pool, but all I saw was Nate Brown lying on that football field, not moving. My stomach churned. Sweat beaded on my forehead. This was my worst nightmare come true.

"Paralysis?" I said, barely getting the word out of my mouth. "How long is it going to last? He will get better, won't he?"

Dr. Stevens looked at me intently. "Like I said, it's too early to tell, Reggie. Often in these cases, the swelling subsides and the feeling comes back. Sometimes the person makes a full recovery. Other times, there is permanent damage to the spinal cord—"

"Permanent damage?" I said. "You mean like he wouldn't get better? Maybe not play football again?"

"Football isn't the important thing here," Dr. Stevens said. "Right now, Nate and his family are worrying about whether he will be able to walk again."

I felt the tears rush to my eyes even though I was fighting them back. "Oh my God."

"Reggie," Dr. Stevens said, "you have to keep this in perspective. What happened on Friday night was a fluke. You had nothing to do with it. From what I remember of the play, you couldn't have seen Nate coming. So don't beat yourself up. Nate is getting the finest care possible. All we can do is hope for the best."

I heard Dr. Stevens's words, but I wasn't listening. Not really. All I could think of was Nate Brown lying in that hospital bed, his family gathered around. His mother wishing I was dead.

chapter six

The walk home from Jeff's house seemed like a long one. I had barely said a word during supper. Afterward, when Jeff asked if I wanted to take a swim, I had quietly declined.

I told him it was because I wasn't feeling well, which was sort of true. But I wasn't sick, just dejected. I had gone to Dr. Stevens hoping for a positive update on Nate Brown. Instead, I had received almost the worst news possible.

I saw the Lincoln spirit sign on the front lawn as I approached our house. It had been there ever since the start of this school year. Members of the pep squad planted them on the lawns of all the varsity football players. Mine was black with white lettering—the Lincoln colors—and it bore my number, 77. Underneath the number were the words *Reggie "Stick-'em" Scott*.

The nickname had come from my reputation as a middle linebacker. I was a hard-hitter. That was the main reason I was a starter for the Lions. There were certainly bigger, faster guys on the team, but nobody hit as hard as me. Usually, the sign stirred a feeling of pride inside me. Tonight it just made me queasy. Who wanted to be known as "Stick-'em" when a kid was lying in a hospital bed?

I grabbed the sign and roughly yanked the metal ends out of the grass. Resisting the temptation to break it over my knee, I walked around to the side of the house and dumped it by the trash cans.

I didn't say much to my parents that night, although I could tell they were concerned about me. At about 9:00 PM, I told them I was going to bed.

"Little early, isn't it?" Dad said, looking up from his newspaper.

"I'm just tired. It's been a long day."

"Come here a minute," Mom said.

I walked over to the kitchen counter, where they were both sitting. Normally, I felt pretty connected to my parents. Right now I didn't think there was much they could do to help me.

"Reggie, I know you're still worried about that boy," Mom said. "But you have to let it go. There's nothing you can do."

"I know. I'll try."

Mom grabbed me and hugged me, kissing my forehead.

"If you need to talk about anything, just let us know, okay?" Dad said.

I nodded. I knew that they were trying to help, but they didn't know how. I didn't know how to help myself, either.

As I headed up the stairs to bed, I hoped that tomorrow things would feel better.

I saw it the second I opened the front door the next morning to grab the newspaper. The Lincoln spirit sign that I had left by the trash cans was back in the front yard. This was weird.

I walked into the kitchen. "This is bizarre," I said. "I put that spirit sign by the trash when I came home last night. Now it's back on the lawn this morning..."

"I put it there," Dad said. "I noticed last night that it had been taken down, and I stuck it back up. Reggie, you've got nothing to feel bad about. You're a Lincoln varsity football player. We're proud of that, and you should be too."

I shook my head. Tears welled up in my eyes. "I took that sign down for a reason," I yelled.

Dad looked hurt. "Reggie, I..."

"Forget it," I said, running out to the lawn and yanking the sign out once again. "I'm getting rid of this stupid thing for good."

I pulled the sign out of the metal holder. Then I held it up in front of me and ripped it in half. I grabbed the pieces, ran around the side of the house and stuffed them deep into the trashcan. The sign wasn't going up again.

I was still angry a few minutes later when Dad confronted me. "What's this all about, Reggie?" he said.

Tears were now streaming down my cheeks, and I let it all out. I told Dad about my talk with Dr. Stevens and about how Nate Brown might never walk again. About how I didn't want to be known as "Stick-'em" anymore.

"I can understand how you must be feeling," he said quietly. "That's really awful news about Nate. But we still don't know how this is going to turn out. Try to be positive. Remember that no matter what anybody says, this really had nothing to do with you."

Somewhere, in the most logical part of my brain, I knew Dad was right. Nate had hit me, not the other way around. It was Nate who had used sloppy, dangerous tackling technique, not me. Maybe if I kept telling myself that over and over, it would start to feel like the truth.

chapter seven

Football practice went a little better over the next couple of days, although I still didn't feel anything like my usual self out on the field. Unlike Monday, we didn't do much hitting with our first-string offense. Coach Clark didn't like risking injury so close to the next game. It was mostly drills and chalk talk as the coaching staff tried to get us ready to face Franklin. The Demons had won their first game of the year 53–0 over

Peabody the previous week. This was a huge game for us. We all knew it.

Just before Thursday's practice, Coach Clark called us all in to midfield. "Take a knee," he said. "I've got some news. First of all, Nate Brown is still in hospital. The doctors say it's too early to tell what his long-term prospects are. For now, he's not walking. I know that's not what anybody wants to hear, but I thought you boys deserved to know the truth."

For most of the players, this was the first news they'd had about Nate Brown. I could sense it was hitting a few of the kids pretty hard.

"Nate is in room three-one-six at Gower General," Coach Clark continued. "He's not allowed visitors yet, but I'm sure the family would appreciate cards or letters. The second piece of news is this: Our game against Milbury has been rescheduled. Instead of a bye in the final week of the regular season, we will now play them, but the game will be at their field. That's all. Now let's get to work."

We divided into offense and defense and began running through drills. It was the day before a game, so Coach Molloy was keeping things pretty light.

"Reggie, can I have a word with you, please?" Coach Molloy said as the first drill began. As I walked over to join him on the sidelines, I noticed him motion to Coach Clark as well.

The three of us sat on the bench while the rest of the team continued to practice. Nobody seemed to notice that I had been pulled away for this meeting.

"Reggie," Coach Clark began, "you haven't had much spark this week, kid, either in your play or your attitude at practice. Is everything okay?"

I couldn't believe that Coach was asking me this after what had happened the week before. Of course everything wasn't okay. A kid was paralyzed.

"Yeah," I mumbled. I was lying. "I mean, yes, sir."

"I don't think you're being straight with us, Reggie," Coach Molloy said. "I've been coaching you for years now. I don't remember a week when you looked like this."

"Looked like what?" I snapped back. "What's wrong with the way I've been playing?"

I immediately regretted my tone. But it was too late to take it back. I was just so sick of people constantly asking me what was wrong.

"Well, you haven't been yourself," said Coach Clark. "For one thing, you haven't been hitting anything like the 'Stick-'em' of old." Suddenly, I loathed that nickname more than anything in the world.

"I think it's got something to do with the Brown kid," Coach Molloy said. "Am I right, Reggie? Is that still in your head?"

I nodded. Was it that obvious?

"I can't help thinking about him, Coach," I said. "I can't help thinking that if I had just done something different. If I had just—"

"Reggie, I'm going to tell you this for the last time," Coach Clark said, his voice growing stern. "You had absolutely nothing to do with that boy getting injured."

"Then why does it feel that way?" I blurted out. "Why can't I get the picture of him lying there out of my head? Why can't I concentrate on plays? It's all I think about in school and at home—all the time."

The coaches looked at each other. Coach Clark spoke first.

"Son, I've been watching you very closely in practice," he said. "I think it's best if you don't play tomorrow. Your head's just not there yet, Reggie. And I don't want *you* getting hurt."

"But, Coach...," I began.

"I've made my decision," he said. "Just hit the showers now, take the weekend off football."

"You're kicking me off the team! Coach, that's not fair."

"No, Reggie," Coach Clark said firmly. "We're certainly not kicking you off the team. You're an important part of Lincoln football. But you can't play safely or effectively the way you are right now.

"We've spoken with your parents. We all agree. We want you to see a sports psychologist. Dr. Stevens knows a good one. He thinks it will help."

A sports psychologist? What, was I crazy now too? My parents and the coaches had been talking about me behind my back and making decisions for me. Everything was spinning out of control.

"Come see me Monday," Coach Clark said gently. "We'll talk again then."

I walked off the field, stunned. Although I hadn't exactly been pumped to play tomorrow night, the thought of not playing was even worse. If I had felt alone with my problems before, that feeling was now magnified a thousand times.

I slowly peeled off my pads in the locker room and changed into my sweatpants and flip-flops. Now, as well as wondering if Nate Brown would ever play football again, I was wondering about my own future in the game too.

I noticed the Bronco in the school parking lot as I started to walk home from practice. That was strange. What was Dad doing here?

He honked the horn and motioned me over to the SUV. I opened the passenger door and jumped in.

"Coach told me I'd be able to find you here," he said. "Thought you'd want to talk to somebody."

"Seems like you've already done plenty of talking," I replied. "Seems like you and the coaches already have everything decided for me."

Dad turned off the ignition and took his hands off the steering wheel. "Reggie, we're only doing what's best for you."

"What's best for me?" I interrupted, growing angrier by the second. "So what's best for me is missing a big football game in my senior season? And going to see a shrink? Is that best for me too?"

"We think so," Dad said softly. "Let's face it, Reg, you haven't been yourself this week. That's understandable. Something like this is traumatic. Sometimes people need help to work through it."

"I don't need any help!" I screamed. "And I don't need a ride, either. I'm walking home."

I slammed the car door as I got out. Dad didn't try to stop me. But he pulled up alongside me, rolled down the passenger-side window and said, "Cool off some on your way home. We'll talk later."

"Whatever," I said, without looking at him. Deep down I knew I wasn't mad at my father. But I felt like I had to take my anger and frustration out on somebody.

I walked home slowly, with everything swirling in my head. If this hadn't been the worst day of my life, it had come awfully close.

chapter eight

I kept quiet during dinner that night, barely listening as Mom and Dad discussed everything except high school football. As I munched on Mom's meatloaf, I felt guilty about how I had spoken to Dad at the school, but I didn't want to bring it up. I was just hoping for a nice quiet evening and a good sleep. Maybe that would help make things clearer.

No such luck. "I'll clear the dishes," Mom said. "And you two talk."

The way she said it, I knew Dad wanted to have a serious discussion. Normally all three of us cleared the dishes, cleaned up the kitchen and loaded the dishwasher. Mom was obviously trying to make sure Dad and I patched things up.

"Reggie, I'm sorry you feel we ganged up on you," Dad began.

My anger had subsided a bit, but I still wasn't happy about having to sit out against Franklin. Playing the Demons was supposed to be one of the highlights of my senior season. But even I had to admit that part of me didn't feel much like playing football.

"You guys are just trying to help me. I know," I said wearily. "But how can I miss the Franklin game? It's one of the biggest of the year."

"I agree with Coach," Dad said solemnly. "You're not ready to play football. He said you've been avoiding contact in practice, and that your head just hasn't been in the game this week. We've noticed that you're not really yourself around home, either."

I didn't reply. I just stared down at the dining room table.

"Reggie, I've got a referral from Dr. Stevens," Dad continued. "He wants you to go see Jim MacIntyre. He's a sports psychologist who has helped lots of kids in similar situations. Maybe he'll be able to help you too."

"I don't need a shrink," I said curtly. "Do you guys think I'm nuts, or what?"

"No, Reggie, we don't think you're nuts," Dad said slowly. "But sometimes things affect us in ways we aren't even aware of. Lots of people see therapists. Look at it this way: You're going to be getting some expert help—no different than if you sprained an ankle or broke your leg."

Yeah, right. Nobody thought you were a wacko if you went to the doctor. But just wait until the kids at Lincoln found out I was seeing a psychologist.

"That's easy for you to say," I blurted out. "Nobody's ever told you that you need this kind of help, have they?"

My father's brow furrowed. He sighed and shook his head slowly. Maybe my last comment had gone too far.

"I've never told you this before, Reggie," he said. "I *have* needed that kind of help myself."

I was stunned. What was he talking about? My Dad, the most dependable, straightforward, no-nonsense Mr. Boring Guy had gone to a therapist?

"A couple of years ago, I had some problems. I had an anxiety disorder," Dad said. "It was different from what you're experiencing. But it was affecting me at home and at work. And just like you, I didn't want to talk to anybody about it. Mom finally convinced me to see somebody."

For a moment I forgot all about my problems and thought about what I was hearing. My Dad had problems with anxiety? How come? Why hadn't I noticed anything? Was he okay now?

"So what happened?" I asked, croaking out the words. "With your, um, problem."

I didn't want to use the term anxiety disorder. I didn't even really know what it meant.

"I went to see Dr. Shaw about it," Dad said, referring to our family doctor. "He put me on some medication. But he also sent me to a therapist. Mostly, we talked about how I was feeling and the problems I was experiencing. He taught me some ways of dealing with the feelings I was having. I know it sounds corny, but it changed my life."

"But how were you feeling?" I had to ask.

"It's hard to explain, but I'll try." He paused and took a deep breath. "I guess the best way to describe it was that I was worried. All the time, about everything. I've always been kind of a worrywart—you know how you and Mom always tease me? But it was beginning to take over my life. I was worried about things that it wasn't logical to be concerned about. I can see that now, but then..."

"Like what?" I asked. This was fascinating and scary at the same time.

"Like, for instance, I'd drive through an intersection and then, thirty seconds later, start wondering if the light had really been green when I'd driven through. Then I would wonder if I'd caused an accident. I'd worry about something like that all day. It started to affect my work, and I wasn't sleeping well or eating right. I was always worrying about something. When it was at its worst, I was barely functioning."

"I never knew," I said, shaking my head.

"People with mental health issues are pretty good at hiding them until it becomes extreme," Dad said. "That's when they usually get help—when it gets so bad they are finally forced into seeing somebody."

I was in a daze as my father continued talking. I was absorbing his words but I was also worried: What if I had inherited Dad's problem? What he had described to me sounded pretty scary.

It was as if he was reading my mind. Dad looked directly at me now and put his hand on my shoulder. "I know what's bothering you is different from what I went through," he said. "You need help dealing with the aftereffects of one traumatic incident. For me it was a chronic condition, something that built up over time. But I also know that if you don't get some help, it can wreck things for you too. You don't want that."

I shook my head. "No," I said slowly, "I guess not."

Still, the thought of seeing a psychologist made me nervous. What would people think about me?

"I know that it seems like a strange thing, seeing a therapist," Dad said, again echoing my thoughts. "But it's not, really. I mean, when you think about it, your mind is one of the most important parts of your body. It affects everything."

When he put it that way, it made sense. I was looking at Dad in a whole different light than I had just a few minutes ago.

"Okay," I said.

"Okay, what?"

"I'll go see him. This psychologist."

A wide smile spread across my father's face, and his blue eyes twinkled. "That's great, Reg," he said. "I think you're making the right decision."

I went to bed that night with a bunch of different thoughts racing through my mind. I wondered what it would be like to talk to somebody about what was going through my mind—my private thoughts. I still felt a little uncomfortable about sharing them.

I wondered how Nate Brown was doing, lying in a hospital bed. He was probably a lot more uncomfortable than me, thinking about whether he was ever going to walk—let alone play football—again. Maybe talking to someone about my feelings wasn't such a big deal.

But mostly, as I tried to get to sleep, I thought about my father. Dad and I had always had a good relationship, but our conversation tonight was the most open he had ever been with me. Part of me felt good that he trusted me enough to tell me those things. But another part felt scared that my Dad, who had always been a rock in my life, had experienced something so frightening. And I hadn't even noticed there was anything wrong.

chapter nine

Another big surprise was awaiting me the next morning at breakfast, as I dug into the Friday *Times* with my bowl of Cheerios.

Even though I wasn't playing in tonight's game against Franklin, I still flipped quickly to the prep sports section.

Division mulling suspension for Lincoln player read the headline atop the small story on the right side of page three. A queasy feeling crept into my stomach, and I stopped chewing my cereal.

Northeast Athletic District officials are considering a Milbury request for disciplinary action against a Lincoln player following a serious spinal injury to Miners tight end Nate Brown.

A *district source has informed the* Times *that a number of complaints have been made about the play on which Brown was injured last week. The Milbury player remains in Gower General Hospital.*

I couldn't believe what I was reading. Were they serious? I hadn't done anything on the play except get hit. Or had I? Was there something on the game video that showed something different? Something I'd missed? Now my stomach was really flipping about.

I read on. *The Lincoln player involved in the incident was linebacker Reggie Scott, a senior with a reputation for being a hard hitter in the defensive backfield.*

What were they talking about in this story? I hadn't hit anybody on that play. It had been the other way around. But this article was making it look like I had laid out Nate Brown with a vicious tackle. This was unfair. So why was it making me feel guilty?

There was just one more paragraph to the story: *District officials were tight-lipped about a possible suspension. But it appears Scott will play tonight when the Lions take on the highly rated Franklin Demons in one of the most anticipated games of the season.*

I tossed the paper across the eating bar in disgust. The story made me sound like some kind of dirty player, like it was my fault Nate was lying in a hospital bed. How could they put something like that in the newspaper without even checking the facts?

Dad looked up from his section of the *Times* after I threw the Sports section down. "Everything okay?" he asked.

"This is unreal," I said. "They're saying I'm going to be suspended."

Dad dropped his part of the paper and grabbed the Sports section. He quickly found the article, scanned it for a few seconds and then put it down. "Irresponsible," he muttered. I could tell he was choked.

"This is a terrible piece of journalism," he said. "It seems to be based on a rumor and not on any fact. I'm sure you won't be suspended. You did nothing wrong. But I will call the *Times* today to complain. And I will call Coach Clark."

I nodded. The story was already in the newspaper, though. Even though it wasn't true, people would assume it was. That was just the way things worked.

The school day that followed was one of the strangest that I had ever experienced at Lincoln. It was a football Friday, so there was the usual hoopla. The Lions pep squad was selling "Defeat the Demons!" ribbons during the morning break. All the players, including me, were wearing our Lincoln jerseys to class.

At lunchtime, there was the usual pep rally in the gym with a couple of hundred students sitting in the bleachers. The cheerleading team turned cartwheels and built human pyramids out on the hardwood. Coach Clark stepped to the microphone and talked about how important this game was to our season. I hardly heard a word he said.

My mind was elsewhere. I wasn't playing tonight, and it felt weird. Normally, on a game day, I would get more and more excited as each class ended, itching to get out on the field. Today, I just felt tired. I was sad I wouldn't be playing, but in another way I was relieved. Everything about the day felt off.

The last buzzer had just rung, and I was walking toward my locker when Jeff Stevens called out from behind. "Hey, Stick-'em. You ready to kick some serious Franklin butt?"

I knew Jeff was just being friendly, but I didn't want to hear that nickname. Not now or ever. I didn't want to talk to anybody about football, either.

"Not really," I said quietly. "I'm not playing tonight."

Jeff's jaw fell and his blue eyes opened wide in surprise. "What are you talking about, dude?" he said. "That story in the paper this morning was bogus. Everybody knows that."

"I can't play," I repeated solemnly. "The coaches and my parents decided I wasn't ready to suit up."

"Not ready?" Jeff said, dumbfounded. "What's wrong with you? Are you injured?"

"Not exactly."

"What does 'not exactly' mean?" Jeff said. "You're acting weird, man."

I turned and faced Jeff, shaking my head. "Look, I can't explain it, okay?" My voice was rising, and I felt my forehead growing hot. "It's not my choice. You'll have to ask Coach—and maybe your dad—why I'm not suiting up."

Jeff was really confused now. "My dad? What does my dad have to do with anything?"

"I'm just not playing, okay?" I was really annoyed now, and my voice was breaking. "Good luck tonight."

"What do you mean, 'good luck?'" Jeff said. "You'll be there, right?"

"I don't know," I said, backing away quickly down the hall. "It's just too weird. I'll talk to you later."

I had to get out of there, away from Jeff. I was getting too emotional and I couldn't explain why. I wanted more than anything else to be with my teammates but I knew deep down that I wasn't ready to play. And I wasn't ready to tell them why.

The six-block walk home seemed even stranger than the rest of the school day. Normally, on a football Friday, I stayed at school and ate a pre-game meal with the team in the cafeteria. Then we went over plays and strategies with the coaches and slowly got dressed for the pre-game warm-up. Tonight, I was heading home.

The coaches had intercepted me first thing that morning at school to tell me that the newspaper story was wrong. There wouldn't be any suspension. They had also asked me to spend the afternoon and evening with the team, just like normal. But I didn't feel right doing that. If I'd been wearing a cast on my leg or had my arm in a sling, it might have been okay. Those things were almost expected for a football player. But what was I supposed to do now? Wrap my head up in a big bandage? I had no way to explain to the guys on the team that I wasn't playing because of a mental problem.

"Reggie, I'm surprised to see you," Mom said as I came in through the back door. "Why aren't you with the team? You guys have Franklin tonight, right?"

"I couldn't do it," I said glumly. "I just don't feel like I belong there today."

Mom walked over to me and wrapped me in a big hug. Although I was now at least five inches taller and twenty pounds heavier than her, I still felt like a little kid whenever she hugged me. It still made me feel better too.

"I understand," Mom said soothingly. "This is a tough thing you're going through."

Mom broke away from me and hurried over to the stove. "Sorry," she said. "I have to stir this chili or it'll burn in the bottom of the pot.

"I'll tell you what," she continued. "When Dad gets home, we can all have some of this. Then we'll go to the game together. It's not every game I get to sit with my boy."

I smiled weakly. "I don't know," I said. "I'm not sure I want to go tonight."

"Well, you think it over. Let us know."

"Okay." I nodded. I was suddenly feeling very tired. I went upstairs to my room, flipped on my stereo and plopped down on the bed.

I must have dozed off because it seemed like just a couple of seconds later, Dad was knocking at my bedroom door. He poked his head inside and smiled.

"Hey, Reg," he said. "Are you coming down to have some supper with us?"

I got up and rubbed my eyes. "Be right down."

Mom and Dad were already eating when I sat down at the dining room table. I dug into the big bowl of chili that Mom had laid out for me. Even though it had been a terrible day, the chili, topped with grated cheddar cheese and accompanied by garlic toast, tasted great. It felt good to get some comfort food in my stomach. I hadn't been eating too much the last few days.

"Do you guys still want to catch the game?" I asked.

"If you do," Dad said. "I think it would be good for you to go, but we'd understand if you didn't want to. This must be a pretty weird Friday for you."

"It is," I said. "But I think I should go. I'm a co-captain. Even if I'm not playing, I should be there."

I could tell my decision made Mom and Dad happy. Even though I was the one who put on the uniform every week, both of them really enjoyed the whole Lincoln football experience too. I was pretty sure they would have been disappointed if we'd all stayed home for what was possibly the biggest game of the year.

On the way to the stadium, I tapped Mom on the shoulder from the backseat. "No offense, Mom," I said. "But I don't think I'll sit with you guys. As long as I'm here, I should be down on the field."

Mom grinned. "I'm deeply hurt," she said. "But I'll get over it."

I knew from the lack of noise as I entered the locker room that the coaches were already delivering their pre-game message.

I rounded the corner into the main dressing room area, just in time to hear the last of Coach Clark's speech. "People, I know we're shorthanded out there on defense tonight without Reggie, but Bryce is ready to fill in. Help him out there. Be good teammates, stick together, play Lincoln football."

I looked across the locker room at Bryce Clark, an eleventh grader who was the head coach's son. Bryce was a good player, but he was being pushed into a starting spot because of my absence. I hoped he wasn't feeling too much pressure. At the same time, I felt some resentment. He was taking my spot tonight, the spot I'd worked like a dog to earn since well before I got to Lincoln. And this was the biggest game of the season. It just wasn't fair.

As Coach ended his speech, the players began to chant, "Lions, Lions, Lions." It was our usual ritual before we headed out the locker room door, through the paper Lincoln banner and onto the turf. They were all so focused on the task at hand that nobody noticed me slip in. Nobody except Coach Molloy, that is.

He winked at me. "Good to see you, Reggie. I was hoping you'd come out tonight."

I didn't know what to say in return. But Coach Molloy's words made me feel a little less awkward about being in the locker room without a uniform.

I followed the rest of the guys onto the field, walking with Coach Molloy, just behind Coach Clark. The stands were packed and the stadium lights illuminated the turf. The Lincoln and Franklin bands were taking turns running through fight songs, each trying to outdo the other. Even though I wasn't playing, I still felt jacked just being out there. Who wouldn't on a Friday night like this?

I heard somebody calling my name, and I turned around. Blake Marshall, a friend from chemistry class, was motioning me over to the stands.

"That sucks about your suspension," Blake said matter-of-factly.

"What?"

"Your suspension," he repeated. "For that hit on the Milbury kid."

"I'm not suspended," I said firmly. "And I didn't hit that kid. He—"

Blake didn't let me finish my sentence. "Not suspended? That's what the paper said, dude. How come you're not dressed then?"

My face flushed. I didn't know how to answer that. "Injury," I mumbled. "See you, man. I gotta go."

I returned to the sidelines, shaken by the conversation. If Blake thought I was suspended, then lots of other people must be thinking the same thing. I wished they would make an announcement on the PA system saying that I wasn't suspended. But then what would they say?

"Number seventy-seven, Reggie 'Stick-'em' Scott, is not playing tonight due to mental problems." Yeah, right. I was better off with people thinking I'd been suspended.

Lincoln won the coin toss and elected to receive. Sammy Price, Franklin's kicker, sent the ball deep to begin the game, straight into the hands of Jeff Stevens. That was good for us. Jeff has size and good hands, but he also has deceptive speed for a big guy. The Demons had likely kicked the football his way because they didn't want the smaller quicker Ronnie Bright to catch the ball. I was hoping Jeff would make them pay for that choice.

Sure enough, Jeff caught the football on the dead run and headed to the outside at full speed. He found a couple of blocks early and managed to get all the way to midfield before being brought down by Sammy Price. If not for that one tackle, Jeff would have gone all the way.

His return was enough to get us off to a terrific start. Lance Turner, our starting quarterback, had looked unbeatable in practice. He carried that into the game. Three plays after the opening kick, Lance and Jeff Stevens were already celebrating a touchdown after the quarterback completed a twenty-yard strike down the middle to my best buddy. Even though I wasn't out there with them, my heart soared as Jeff crossed the goal line. This was an awesome start for us.

But things evened out in a hurry. The Demons were conference co-favorites along with Lincoln, and we quickly found out why. Vince Poynter, their starting quarterback, was a tall fluid athlete who could run and throw with equal ease. Whenever we bottled him up inside, Poynter dropped back in the pocket and delivered an accurate pass. And whenever we tried to get more pressure on his throws, he seemed to find daylight outside, running for big gains.

Our offense was clicking too. The game evolved into a terrific seesaw battle. With four minutes remaining in the fourth quarter, we trailed Franklin 28–24 with the ball in our possession at our own twenty-five yard line. "Time-out!" Coach Clark yelled. We all huddled around him.

"Okay, guys, this is it," Coach said, scanning the eyes in the huddle. "This is where we see what kind of character you have."

The coach paused and let his words sink in before continuing. "Lance, I want you to run the L Series. Get out of bounds to stop the clock whenever you can. Protect the ball. No fumbles. Okay? Let's make this happen, gentlemen."

All the players stuck their right hands into the middle of the huddle. "One-two-three, Lions!" we yelled.

The L Series was a sequence of plays we ran whenever we needed a score in the dying minutes of a game. It was a series of short passing routes and running plays. Lance usually threw quick patterns to Jeff, pitched out to Ronnie Bright or ran himself. They were our three most dependable offensive players. It was a good plan on Coach's part.

Meanwhile, Franklin's huge defensive line dug in to try and stop the Lincoln drive. I could hear them taunting Lance as he bent over to take the snap. "Comin' for you, Turner," one yelled. "Gonna be a Turner-over," screamed another.

Lance ignored them and confidently called out the signals. He took the snap, dropped back two steps and nailed Jeff on a quick crossing pattern. First down. That shut up the wise guys on the other side of the ball.

Six plays later, we were at the Franklin twenty-five, knocking on the door with our crowd getting louder and louder. Lance turned, looked at Coach Clark and made the shape of a triangle with both his hands. Coach nodded. I knew what was coming next.

The triangle was the signal that we had arranged to use during this game for our "special"—the one play our coaches felt could beat the Franklin defense for a long gain. We had saved the special for just such a moment, facing second-down-and-ten with just under two minutes left.

Lance dropped back and put the football at his side. It appeared he was going to hand it off to fullback Dexter Bart, who was steaming up the middle. I could see the Franklin defensive linemen and linebackers caught in mid-step, not knowing how to react to what looked very much like it was going to be a running play.

The deception was enough to throw the Demons off for just a split second. Lance deftly pulled the football back up to his shoulder just as Bart raced past him. As the quarterback rolled out quickly to his right, he scanned downfield to where Jeff Stevens was streaking toward the end zone.

Hot on Lance's heels was a crush of three Franklin defenders. It looked as though they were going to catch him for a big loss. But just as they converged, he unloaded the football. As it hung in the air, the entire stadium seemed to hold its breath.

In the end zone, Jeff Stevens was being closely pursued by Franklin defensive back Curt Hodges. Both players leaped to meet the ball. When they came down, Jeff had the football tucked in his arms. He sprang up quickly, raising his hands above his head. The crowd roared. Kyle Nance, our ninth-grade kicker, booted the extra point. Lincoln led 31–28 with only ninety seconds remaining.

Coach Clark quickly huddled us on the sidelines. "Okay, guys. The offense did its job. Now it's up to the D. Let's go win this football game."

Once again, the team ran through its cheer, and our guys took the field. Nance sent the kickoff high and deep to Vince Poynter at the Demons' ten yard line. Poynter managed to avoid a couple of early tackles to get outside and use his long, easy stride to reach the Franklin forty-five yard line before being brought down by a gang of Lincoln special-teamers.

There were now only eighty seconds remaining on the clock. Franklin still had a chance, but it would be able to get off only three or four plays before the fourth quarter ended. I was confident that our defense was up to the task. Suddenly, I wished I was out on the field with the rest of the guys, fighting for this big win.

I noticed immediately that Franklin had lined up slightly differently with its backs deeper behind the line. In a second, I knew why. Vince Poynter dropped back five yards behind his center and called for the snap. The Demons were going into the shotgun formation for the first time in the game.

The long snap gave Poynter the time he needed to get outside our rush and find the sidelines. By the time we had brought down the graceful Franklin quarterback, he had crossed midfield.

The Demons remained in the shotgun the rest of the game. But after the initial surprise factor, it didn't work nearly as well. With the clock down to twenty-five seconds, Franklin found itself in a desperate fourth-and-ten situation with the ball at our forty. It was too far for a field goal, so the Demons had no choice but to make one last stab at a first down.

Poynter dropped back once again, taking the long snap. But this time, he didn't head to the outside or throw the football. Instead, he faked left and ran straight up the middle. It was a naked quarterback draw, and Bryce Clark was in a perfect position to bring down the Franklin quarterback.

Clark rushed toward Poynter, ready to make the tackle. I could almost feel his heart beating as he zeroed in on the quarterback. He could end the game with this one hit. It was that simple.

Except for one problem. As Clark rushed toward Poynter, the smooth Franklin pivot juked with his hips and stuttered his step ever so slightly. The motion was just enough to cause Clark to mistime his tackle. He missed his target altogether. As Poynter squirted by the fallen Lincoln middle linebacker for a key first down, I heard the crowd groan. If the Lincoln stadium had been a gigantic balloon, this missed tackle was a devastating pinprick.

Bryce Clark was still lying on the field after Poynter was finally hauled down at our twenty-five. I felt badly for him. He was the coach's son, so he took enough heat just for that. But tonight the eleventh-grader had been asked to fill a very difficult position against an extremely good team.

Poynter's first down meant it had all come down to one play. Franklin needed a field goal—about a thirty-five-yarder, including the snap distance—to tie the game. There was only time for one more play before the fourth quarter expired. Sammy Price, the Demons' senior kicker, trotted confidently onto the field.

The teams lined up. It seemed like an eternity before the ball was actually snapped. It went to Poynter, who pinned it perfectly and allowed Price to lay a solid boot into it. Again, the crowd was quiet as the ball sailed toward the uprights. I hoped desperately that it would sail wide or fall short. But Price was an all-district kicker. The ball split the uprights cleanly. The horn sounded to end the game. We had tied Franklin 31-31. So why did it feel so much more like a loss?

chapter ten

The disappointing way that the Franklin game had ended bothered me, but not as much as the other news hanging over me all weekend. Dad had delivered it casually on Saturday morning.

"You'll have to miss some school Monday morning," he said. "Dr. MacIntyre's office called today. It's great he can see you so soon."

Yeah, great, I thought. On Monday, some-one was going to start dissecting my brain.

All weekend, I thought about little else. What kinds of questions was he going to ask me? Would he hypnotize me like some of those quacks on TV? I wasn't feeling too comfortable about it at all.

Dad must have sensed my mood at dinner Sunday night. After we had all cleaned up, he asked me if I wanted to shoot a few hoops down at Tipton Park.

We'd been shooting for just a couple of minutes when Dad grabbed the ball and put it on his hip. "Are you nervous about seeing Dr. MacIntyre?" he asked.

"I guess. Were you nervous when you asked for help?"

"I wasn't so much nervous as I was a total wreck," Dad said. "But I'll tell you, after talking about it with somebody once, I felt a hundred percent better.

"Just go in there with an open mind," he continued. "He's not going to be performing weird experiments on you or anything like that. You're going to be talking, like we are now."

I hoped he was right. I went to sleep that night stewing about my appointment, but the next morning, I felt a little better. I figured if Dad could do it, so could I.

Mom drove me to the Gower Medical Center where Dr. MacIntyre had his office. It was about twenty minutes from home and right beside Gower General. She dropped me off there before heading to work. After my appointment, I planned to take a city bus to school. If everything went according to plan, I might be able to get to Lincoln for third-period math. Oh joy.

As I walked toward the clinic entrance, I stared up at the third floor of Gower General, wondering which room Nate Brown was in. I tried to push the thought out of my mind as I headed through the glass doors and reported to the receptionist.

I'd only been waiting for about three minutes when an athletic-looking man in his forties with sandy brown hair came into the waiting area. He smiled at me. "Reggie," he said. "Come on in."

We shook hands at the doorway. "I'm Reggie Scott," I said. "But I guess you knew that already."

"Middle linebacker for Lincoln, right?" the psychologist replied. "You're quite a player."

"Thanks, Dr. MacIntyre," I said. "But not so much lately."

Dr. MacIntyre ignored my last comment and smiled. "You can just call me Jim," he said. "We like to keep things informal around here."

As I stepped into the room, I couldn't help but notice that it looked more like a sports hall of fame than my idea of a psychologist's office. There wasn't a couch or anything even remotely medical. There were a few overstuffed leather chairs and a whole lot of trophies and pictures—some showing a young football player and his teammates, others showing the same young man on a basketball court.

"You're probably wondering about all the pictures and souvenirs," Jim said.

"I'm a sports nut. Played every sport I could when I was a kid. I just can't seem to bring myself to get rid of all this stuff. My wife doesn't want it at home, so I keep it here.

"Besides," he continued, "it kind of fits in with what I do here. There are a lot of good psychologists out there, Reggie, but I focus specifically on sports. A lot of people thought I was crazy when I told them I was going to specialize in working with athletes, but I'm so busy, I have to turn patients away. It's a big field, if you'll excuse the pun."

I laughed at his lame joke. I hoped his treatment was better than his sense of humor.

"Anyway, what we try to do here is help people find out what's stopping them from achieving their best performance," he said. "We identify what's bothering them. Then we teach them ways of coping with those things so they can reach their potential.

So I guess the first thing I have to ask is this: What's bothering you, Reggie?"

I gulped. I guessed I'd better just get it out there. This was what I was here for.

"Well, I don't know if I actually need to be here or not," I said, hedging a little. "But my coaches think I do, and my parents think I do, so I guess I do."

"Well, Reggie," Dr. MacIntyre said. "This is only going to work if you want help. If you're here just to satisfy somebody else, you might as well not waste your time or mine."

"I guess I do need some help." The second I said it, I felt a little weight come off my shoulders. Dad had been right.

I spent a little while telling Dr. MacIntyre about the game against Milbury: how I hadn't even seen Nate Brown until he made contact with me. I told him about celebrating the interception before I realized that Nate was seriously injured. I told him how angry Nate's mom had been with me that day at Gower General.

"So why do you suppose your coaches asked you to come see me?" Dr. MacIntyre asked.

"They say I haven't been hitting well in practice, that I'm not myself out there. They say they're worried about me getting hurt."

"What do you think, Reggie?"

"I guess they're right," I said. "I mean, every time I draw a bead on a kid to tackle him, I think of Nate lying in the hospital. Then something happens. I can't hit hard or sometimes even at all. For some reason, I let up."

"What do you suppose causes that?" Dr. MacIntyre asked.

"Well, I don't really know. I guess I'm still freaked out by what happened. I don't want something like that to happen again, maybe. And I don't want to keep feeling responsible for Nate."

"That's a great start, Reggie," Dr. MacIntyre said. "We're going to have to wrap it up for today. I'd like you to come and see me at the same time Wednesday morning. Does that work for you?"

I was surprised the session was already over. We hadn't solved anything but, as I looked at the clock on my way out of the reception area, I realized I'd been in there for nearly an hour.

I don't know quite how it happened or when I decided to do it. I had been planning to head straight for the bus stop and catch the bus that would take me to school.

But as I left the medical center, I took one look at Gower General and realized that I had to go there instead. If Nate Brown was still in there, I had to make another attempt to see him.

I was already familiar with the hospital layout, so I bypassed the lobby and headed straight for the elevator. When the doors opened on the third floor, I proceeded to the head nurse's station. I just hoped that I didn't run into Nate's mother again.

The nurse on duty was the same woman with jet-black hair and hazel eyes that I had met the last time. She seemed to recognize me.

"He's not here," she said softly, before I could even ask for Nate's room number.

My face dropped. Not here? What did that mean? Oh, God. It couldn't mean that he was...

The nurse's warm smile calmed me. "Don't worry," she said. "He's doing much better. He's in recovery. He's not in the ICU anymore."

"What does 'in recovery' mean?" I asked. I felt completely at her mercy. Every bit of information she had about Nate was like precious gold to me.

Instead of answering me, she said, "You're the boy who was here before, aren't you?"

I nodded, half expecting her to kick me out in the next breath.

"I felt so bad about what happened last week," she said. "You didn't deserve to be treated like that. His mom was so stressed out, she didn't know what she was saying."

I wasn't so sure about that. I had felt the hatred in Mrs. Brown's stare that day. I didn't want to feel that ever again.

"So, how is he doing?" The words clogged my throat. I wanted so much for the news to be good.

"He's getting better. He's got some movement back in his legs. The doctors are hopeful that, as the swelling on his spine goes down, he will get more and more mobility back. With lots of hard work in physiotherapy, he could make a full recovery."

A full recovery? I sat down in the chair next to the nurse's desk. My legs felt weak. This news was so good, so welcome, that I was numb all over.

"Do you want to see him?" the nurse asked. "I might be able to arrange it."

"For sure," I said. "I mean, yes, if that's okay."

The nurse picked up the phone and dialed some numbers. "Hello, this is Harrison from ICU. Is Nathaniel Brown awake right now? Oh, good. I'm sending a friend down to see him. All right then. Thank you."

The nurse turned to me with a smile. "It's your lucky day. He's awake, and his Mom isn't here. Poor thing. She went home to get some sleep this morning. She hasn't had much of that since this happened."

The nurse told me to go to the fifth floor and ask at the desk there. I could see Nate for a few minutes before his next round of medication.

I turned to leave, and then I turned back. "I just wanted to say thanks for helping me," I said to the nurse. "I never introduced myself. I'm Reggie."

"Nice to meet you, Reggie." She smiled. "I'm Brenda Harrison. I had a good feeling about you. I'm so happy you came back."

chapter eleven

I rode alone in the elevator to the hospital's fifth floor. I was nervous. I didn't know what to expect when I got to Nate's room. And I was anxious about the possibility of running into his friends or, worse yet, his mom.

As Brenda Harrison had instructed, I went to the head nurse's station on the fifth floor. I asked the older woman at the desk where I could find Nate Brown.

"Nathaniel is in room five," she said. "I'll take you down there."

I followed the nurse down the hall.

"It's right here," she said, pointing to a door. "He has a roommate, and he's pretty tired. So you can only see him for a couple of minutes. And you have to keep the noise down. Okay?"

"Sure," I replied. "Thanks."

I opened the door. The lights were off. There wasn't enough light coming through the lone window to fully illuminate the room. There were two beds, about ten feet apart. A light was on above the far one. I guessed this was Nate's.

My heart was pounding as I crossed the room toward where he lay. Nate was reading a football magazine. He obviously hadn't heard me come through the door. I bumped into a metal cart beside his bed. The noise made him look up from his magazine.

I'm not sure whose face wore more surprise, mine or Nate's. His eyes widened as he looked up. He didn't look sick or hurt—just tired—and he smiled at me.

I had never been so relieved to see a smile in all my life.

"Hey, Reggie." Nate grinned from his bed. "Thanks for coming in to see me."

"Hey," I replied. "I've been really worried about you, dude."

A few seconds of awkward silence followed. "So how are you doing?" I said, finally. "I guess that's a stupid question, huh?"

Nate shook his head. "I'm still pretty messed up," he said. "But I can feel my legs and my feet again. The doctors say that's a really good sign. For a couple of days, it was pretty scary."

He had hardly finished his sentence when I just blurted it out. "Nate, I wanted to say sorry," I said. "I've felt so bad with you lying in here. I wanted to let you know that I didn't mean..."

"Naw," Nate said, shaking his head. "Don't worry about it. It didn't have anything to do with you. I'm the one who—"

The door to the hospital room burst open. In strode Nate's mom.

"What are you doing in here?" she yelled, flashing me the same angry look she had given me last week. "I told you not to come back. We don't need you here!"

"Mom," Nate interrupted. "It's okay. He's my friend. We've been to football camp before. He's just checking to see how I'm doing."

"Friend!" the woman shrieked. "What kind of friend does this to somebody?"

When she said the word "this" she pointed to Nate, lying in the hospital bed. I was feeling sick to my stomach again.

"Stop it, Mom!" Nate yelled. "Reggie didn't have anything to do with this. It was my fault, not his. Why are you doing this?"

I didn't know what to say. I started to back away from Nate's bed. "I'd better be going, anyway," I stammered. "I've got to get to school. Take care, Nate."

The woman had taken a seat in the corner of Nate's room. She had her head buried in her hands. It seemed like she had already forgotten I was there. Nate waved at me and shrugged his shoulders, looking over at his mom and back at me.

I left his room feeling a little better than when I had entered. The fact that Nate's condition was improving was awesome news. He didn't seem the least bit mad at me, which was also a huge relief. His mom, however, was a very different story.

For the entire bus ride to school, all I did was think about what had happened in that hospital room. Nate's Mom had been so upset. I still didn't really understand why.

My detour to the hospital meant that I had missed third-period math. It was lunch hour by the time I arrived at Lincoln. I was heading to the cafeteria to find some of the guys from the team when I heard my name being paged. I was to go to the office. Probably because I'd missed math.

When I got to the office, Coach Clark was there waiting. Beside him was another man, wearing a dark suit and carrying a briefcase.

"Hi, Reggie," Coach said, smiling. "This is Mr. Danton from the Northeast Athletic District office. He wants to speak with us. Can you spare a couple of minutes?"

"Sure."

The three of us walked down to Coach Clark's office. Once inside, the coach pointed each of us to a chair and then closed the door before sitting down.

"Reggie, I'm sure you're curious about what's going on," Mr. Danton said.

I nodded.

"Here's the situation. We've had an official complaint about you from Milbury. It didn't come from the coaches or the players. But the complainant feels that you behaved inappropriately during and after the play on which Nate Brown was injured."

Once again, I felt queasy, and my mouth went dry. Hadn't pretty much everybody been telling me that none of this was my fault?

"I'll be straight with you, Reggie, because you deserve to know," Mr. Danton continued. "The complaint is from Nate's mother, Elizabeth Brown. She feels strongly that something you did on the field caused or helped to cause Nate's injury. And she's particularly upset because she feels you were celebrating after the play. She wants you suspended."

I was speechless.

"We've looked over the video from that play and directly afterward," Mr. Danton continued. "There is no evidence to suggest that you did anything wrong. In fact, the accident was clearly Nate's fault. And it's obvious that what you were celebrating was your interception, not the fact somebody got hurt."

I was relieved to hear that. At least the athletic district believed me.

"Nevertheless," said Mr. Danton, "the district has procedures it must follow. In cases like this, where there is an official complaint, we are compelled to hold a hearing. So that's what I'm here to inform you about, Reggie."

A hearing? Sounded more like a trial to me.

"What for?" I said, my voice squeaking. "I mean, you just said that it was an accident."

Coach Clark interrupted. "Reggie, it's just procedure," he said. "The hearing will be at the athletic district office on Thursday morning at nine AM. It will give you a chance to explain yourself in front of Nate's parents. I'm sure once they hear your side, everything will be fine."

"That's right, Reggie," Mr. Danton said. "You have nothing to worry about here. I'll see you Thursday."

He got up to leave. I said good-bye, and he walked out the door with Coach Clark.

I remained in my chair and mulled over this latest news. Now I understood where the *Times* got the information about a suspension. It had probably come directly from Nate's mom.

I was just leaving the office when Coach Clark returned. "Try to relax, Reggie," he said soothingly. "This will all blow over soon."

I told the coach about going to see Dr. MacIntyre that morning and about how I had popped in to visit Nate Brown. I also told him about my second run-in with Nate's mother.

"That's great news about Nate," the coach said, a wide smile creasing his square face. "That must make you feel better, hey, kid?"

"Yeah, but it didn't feel very good to have his mom screaming at me again," I replied. "She hates me, Coach."

"She doesn't hate you, Reggie. She just hates what's happened to her son. We'll do everything we can at this hearing to smooth things over. In the meantime, let's get you back on the football field this afternoon."

With everything that had gone on this morning, I had forgotten about practice. And all of a sudden, for the first time in more than a week, I realized I was actually looking forward to putting on the pads again.

chapter twelve

By Wednesday morning, my life seemed to be getting back to something approaching normal. Practice had gone okay on Monday and Tuesday. I still wasn't hitting as hard as I usually did, but at least I was hitting again.

My anxiety about Nate Brown had decreased too. Although I was still concerned that he wasn't walking yet, it had been terrific news to hear that he had feeling back in his legs and feet. And the fact that he wasn't angry at me had been a major relief.

On Wednesday morning, when Mom dropped me off at Dr. MacIntyre's office for my second appointment, I wasn't sure what we were going to talk about. Now that Nate was on the road to recovery, I felt better about football. Not completely normal, but better.

"Good morning, Reggie," Dr. MacIntyre said as he called me into his office. The trophies gleamed from behind his desk. One large plaque that hung on the wall behind his chair caught my eye. *Pac-10 Conference Defensive Player of the Year*, it read.

"Did you play football?" I asked. The psychologist had an athletic build, but it had never occurred to me that he might have been a serious football player.

"A little," he said modestly. "I was a middle linebacker for UCLA back in the eighties. I played at Lincoln too. Just like you."

I was blown away. UCLA—that was a big-time college football team. Dr. MacIntyre must have been a great player. It was my dream to get a football scholarship to a school like UCLA.

"That's the position I play too," I said.

"I know, Reggie. I think you and I have a lot in common. In fact, I even went through something like you're going through, back in my freshman year at UCLA. For a couple of weeks, I thought I might even quit football. But I didn't."

"What happened?" I asked. "When you were a freshman, I mean?"

"Nothing happened to me," Dr. MacIntyre said. "It happened to another freshman on our team. He got hit hard in practice by somebody else and tore up his knee. I was right there to see it happen. He never played again. It kind of freaked me out for a while."

Dr. MacIntyre went on to explain that he'd had problems similar to what I'd experienced after that incident. He was shy of contact. He couldn't bring himself to hit hard, even though he'd hit players thousands of times before, and he was afraid of being tackled himself.

"So what did you do to get over that?" I asked.

"I used a technique that one of my coaches suggested," he said. "It's called centering."

"What's that?"

"It involves concentrating on something simple, typically something like deep breathing," Dr. MacIntyre said. "You concentrate on that, and it helps keeps your mind from wandering and dwelling on negative outcomes. Takes a bit of practice, but it works."

It sounded pretty simple. Too simple, in fact. How could breathing deeply help me tackle better and forget Nate Brown's injury?

"Reggie, I'm going to give you some exercises to try," Dr. MacIntyre said. "These are mental exercises tied to a simple physical component. I want you to breathe in deeply, hold the breath for a count of five and then exhale slowly. Try to focus solely on that task and nothing else."

I did what he said. It was easy. This guy might be a psychologist, but this wasn't exactly rocket science.

"Now, do me a favor," Dr. MacIntyre said. "Today at practice, whenever you're lining up for a snap, do this same deep-breathing exercise. Just wipe everything else out of your mind. And practice it at home too. The more you do it, the more effective it becomes."

"Okay, I'll try it," I said. "Is that what you did to get over your problem?"

Dr. MacIntyre nodded. "That's right," he said. "It worked so well for me, I decided to do it for a living."

We both laughed. I felt a lot better about this second visit than I had my first. I was still skeptical about whether this "centering" thing was actually going to work, but I was willing to trust Dr. MacIntyre. After all, he had been an NCAA football star. Wait until I told the guys on the team about this.

As I left the clinic, I had already decided to go visit Nate again. I knew I ran the risk of seeing his mother, but it was worth it. The last visit had done both him and me a lot of good.

This time, I went directly to the fifth floor head nurse's station. The nurse there gave me a warm smile. "He's in rehab today," she said. "His progress over the last forty-eight hours has really been amazing."

The nurse led me down to a room at the far end of the hall. The inside resembled a dance studio, with rows of bars and mirrors on the walls. Inside, patients were being led slowly through walking exercises, using the bars for support.

I spotted Nate at the far end. He was standing up, resting one arm on the bar and shuffling ahead. It was so good to see him on his feet.

"Hey, dude," I said. "Nice to see you up and around."

Nate grinned. I could tell by the sweat

on his brow that he was working hard. "It's a bit weird, having to do this so slowly. But if feels great to be doing anything."

Nate told me that the swelling on his spine had decreased dramatically. He said he had bugged the doctors to let him try to walk. Finally, this morning, they had agreed.

"I told them I wanted to be at football practice by Thursday," he said.

We both knew he was joking. But who cared? A week ago, neither one of us had been in any mood to joke about anything.

I didn't want to ask the question. Luckily, Nate sensed what was on my mind.

"They say I probably will be able to play again," he said. "If my mom lets me, that is. She's not exactly the world's biggest football fan right now."

I laughed nervously. "She's not exactly my biggest fan, either."

Nate looked directly into my eyes. "I'm

sorry about that, Reggie," he said. "I'm her only kid. This has been a nightmare for her. But I'm really sorry she took it out on you."

Nate stretched out his hand and I shook it. It was so good to see him up and moving around that I almost felt like running back to Lincoln instead of taking the bus.

That afternoon at practice, Coach Molloy worked the defense hard. After we had surrendered the game-tying field goal against Franklin, everybody knew the pressure was on us this week in a road game against Filmore. We couldn't afford a loss to the Friars or our playoff hopes would take a nosedive.

"Okay, gentlemen, it's offense against defense," Coach Clark said. "Let's run it full speed today. Hit hard out there, guys. We've got a big game Friday."

I lined up at middle linebacker, waiting for our offense to run its first play. While they huddled around Lance Turner,

I began the routine that Dr. MacIntyre had suggested. I took a deep breath and held it for five seconds. Then I exhaled slowly, thinking of nothing else. I did it again and again.

I was so focused on my centering technique that I was a second slow to react as Turner took the snap and rushed the football directly up the middle. I dove for his legs, but it was too late. He breezed right by me for a big gain.

"Reggie," yelled Coach Molloy. "You're daydreaming out there. Get your head in the game!"

I was embarrassed. So far, Dr. MacIntyre's technique wasn't exactly working wonders.

Still, I tried it again on the next play. I inhaled and held it for five seconds. Then I exhaled, clearing my mind. The ball didn't come my way for a few snaps, so it was difficult to tell if it was working. I was a little more relaxed than I had been during recent practices.

I continued to use the technique before every snap. Half a dozen plays later I was ready when Turner took the snap and dropped back. I was trying to read his body language, figuring out whether this was a pass or a run. Our quarterback started to his right but then looked up the middle where Jeff Stevens was streaking into the flat.

Lance cocked his right arm and fired the ball on a tight line toward Stevens. Jeff stretched out his arms to bring the ball into his body. But my own instincts had taken over. Three feet away from Jeff, I launched my body into a full tackle. The football and I arrived at the same time. It bounced off Jeff's hands and fell to the ground, joining both of us in a heap on the turf.

Jeff sprung up and glared at me. Then a big smile broke out underneath his face guard. "Yah!" he screamed. "That's the old Stick-'em! Nice hit, dude!"

I looked around at my teammates and coaches. Most of them were smiling. I was back, and it felt great.

I used Dr. MacIntyre's technique for the rest of the practice. It was working. I hadn't hit this well since before the incident with Nate Brown. At the end of practice, Coach Molloy and Coach Clark called me over for a talk.

"Now that's more like it, Reggie," Coach Molloy said, beaming.

"Outstanding effort, son," added Coach Clark.

After a week from hell, it felt so good to be comfortable again on the football field and with my coaches. There was just one more hurdle to clear. The hearing with the Northeast Athletic District officials was tomorrow morning.

chapter thirteen

My alarm was set for 7:00 AM, but I woke up at six and couldn't get back to sleep. I decided I might as well head downstairs and get some breakfast.

Dad was already up and nursing a cup of coffee. "You okay?" he asked, eyeing the kitchen clock.

"Yeah, I guess I'm just a little nervous. I don't know what this thing's going to be like."

"It's perfectly natural for you to be nervous," Dad said. "But I think this is just a formality so that the district is seen to be following proper procedure. Anybody with an ounce of sense realizes you've done nothing wrong."

My father's words were reassuring. I was happy he was coming with me this morning. Dad had taken a half day off from his job at the post office to accompany me to the hearing. I felt a lot better knowing he'd be there to back me up.

I carefully buttoned up my blue dress shirt and put on the striped tie that my aunt had given me for Christmas. I kept it permanently tied and hanging on a coat hook in my bedroom, since I didn't know how to tie it yet. I pulled on my black blazer and tan pants and checked myself out in the mirror. I always felt like somebody else whenever I dressed formally. The only other time I wore this outfit was for the preseason Lincoln team booster dinner, when Coach insisted on it.

Dad and I were quiet on the twenty-minute ride to the Northeast Athletic District office. Neither of us had been there before. Neither of us knew quite what to expect.

When we entered the lobby, Mr. Danton greeted us. He smiled. "Good to see you Reggie, Mr. Scott."

We were led into a large boardroom and seated together on one side along with Coach Clark. Seated along the other side of the table were Mr. and Mrs. Brown. Mrs. Brown was looking toward the far end of the room as we took our seats. She seemed to be deliberately avoiding eye contact with us. The Browns were with a man in a dark suit.

"Let's start with some introductions," said Mr. Danton. He pointed to our side of the table. "This is Reggie Scott and his father, William Scott, along with Coach Clark of the Lincoln Lions."

Mr. Danton turned his head toward the other side. "And over here are Elizabeth and

George Brown, Nate's parents. With them is their attorney, Douglas Wald."

Their attorney? What did the Browns need a lawyer for? I had been reasonably confident heading into the hearing, but I felt nervous now.

Mr. Danton introduced half a dozen members of the athletic district's disciplinary committee who were seated around the far end of the table. He then indicated that the Browns should speak first. But neither one of Nate's parents spoke. Their lawyer did.

"The Browns asked for this hearing because they believe that Reggie Scott should be suspended as a result of the play that occurred September thirteenth, in a Northeast Athletic District football game between Milbury and Lincoln," Mr. Wald said, reading from notes in front of him.

"They believe that actions by Reggie Scott during this play resulted or played a significant role in their son, Nathaniel Brown, suffering a serious spinal injury.

Nathaniel Brown remains in hospital and has been unable to resume his high school football career. In fact, until this week, he had no movement in his lower body as a result of his injury.

"We are formally requesting that the Northeast Athletic District move to suspend Reggie Scott for the duration of Nathaniel Brown's recuperation period. In other words, we are saying that Scott should be required to sit out for as long as Nathaniel himself is sidelined."

Sitting beside me, my father shook his head in silence. I was surprised to hear that the Browns still blamed me for what had happened to their son. Hadn't they looked at the videotape or spoken to Nate? He'd have told them that it wasn't my fault.

"Failing such action by the athletic district, and perhaps even irrespective of it, the Browns have informed me that they are considering legal action against Reggie Scott, Lincoln High School and Coach Clark for damages incurred and potential loss of future earnings as a result of the incident."

Now my head was reeling. First they asked for me to be suspended indefinitely? Now they were talking about a lawsuit? A week where things were looking up for me had suddenly turned back toward disaster.

Mr. Danton cleared his throat. "Now that we have heard from the Browns' side of the table, we'd like to hear from your side," he said, looking our way. "Who would like to speak?"

Coach Clark quickly rose to his feet. "I'll start," he said. "With all due respect to Mr. and Mrs. Brown, I can't believe what is going on here," Coach said. "Reggie Scott is a fine player and, more importantly, a fine young man. I have been coaching at Lincoln for twenty years. I can't remember many players, if any, I have been more proud of.

"During those two decades of coaching football—and ten years of playing the game before that—I have learned a lot about tackling. I may not know a lot about legal language, but I know about football technique. I can tell you, without any hint of reservation, that Nate Brown's injury is the result of poor tackling technique. It's that simple. The only part Reggie Scott played in this was that he was hit by Nate on the play. I can't imagine how you must be feeling, Mr. and Mrs. Brown. But I can tell you this: Blaming Reggie for this is just creating a second victim. It's putting a lot of stress on a good kid who doesn't deserve it.

"That's my opinion, for what it's worth. As far as Lincoln's official position on this goes, we disagree completely with any suspension. Period."

The coach sat down and glanced over at me. It had felt good to hear him defend me like that.

Dad stood up next. "Like the coach here, I want to express my sympathies to Mr. and Mrs. Brown," he said. "I can't even guess what your family must have gone through these past several days. I wouldn't wish that on anybody.

"But our family has gone through a lot too. I've watched my boy wracked with guilt all week over an incident for which he can't possibly be blamed. He sat out last week's game against Franklin because of the effect this has had on him. And he's seeing a psychologist to try to get past it.

"My son has been through enough. He doesn't deserve a suspension. And as far as any legal action goes, I can't even begin to address that. It's too ridiculous to comment on."

Dad sat down. I had never heard him speak so forcefully in public. He had made his point firmly but without yelling or being rude to the Browns.

Mr. Danton turned to me. "Reggie, is there anything you want to say?"

I looked back at Dad. "Go ahead, Reggie, if you want," he said quietly.

I rose from my seat. My legs were shaking and my mouth was dry.

"First of all, I just wanted to say to the Browns that I am sorry this happened to Nate," I said. "I never meant to do anything on the field that would result in anybody getting hurt.

"And I wanted to explain that I wasn't celebrating the fact Nate was injured when I was dancing around," I continued. Tears were coming to my eyes now, and I wasn't able to hold them back.

"I was just happy that I'd made an interception. That's why I was dancing around out there." Now I was looking directly at Nate's mom and pleading. "I didn't even know he was hurt until I looked back. I'm sorry if I made you feel worse because of that."

I sat down. Nate's mom still wasn't looking at me, but his father, a burly man with a square jaw, returned my gaze. He mouthed the words "thank you" as he put his arm around his wife to console her.

"Thank you, Reggie," Mr. Danton said. "I believe we've heard everybody's submissions. That concludes the meeting today. The committee will review the information and come to a decision. Given the tight time frame with league games resuming tomorrow, we will render a decision within twenty-four hours."

We got up from our side of the table. The Browns remained in their seats. As we left the boardroom, George Brown's arm was on his wife's shoulders. Her head remained buried in her arms.

chapter fourteen

It was difficult getting to sleep that night with so many thoughts running through my head. Football practice had gone great that week. Armed with my newfound "centering" strategy from Dr. MacIntyre, I felt like I was playing better than ever. But at the same time, I didn't know whether I'd even be able to suit up the next night for the game against Filmore. Or for the rest of the season, for that matter. There was still a chance I'd be under district suspension.

As much as I had worried about Nate Brown over the last couple of weeks, the thought of not being able to finish my senior football season was devastating.

Sleep finally came, but it wasn't all that restful. I dreamed that I was lying in my bed, trying to get up. But for some reason, I couldn't. My legs just wouldn't move and, as I reached out with my arms to pull myself up, I grabbed onto a metal rail. It was then I realized that I wasn't in my own bed, but in a hospital. I started to panic and scream out for help before I woke up with sweat on my forehead.

I glanced at the clock. It was 6:30 AM. Might as well get up. There would be no going back to sleep today.

The Northeast Athletic District had promised a decision within twenty-four hours. I knew I'd find out sometime today whether I'd be able to play against Filmore, but I wasn't sure exactly when.

After eating breakfast, I walked quickly to school, heading straight for Coach Clark's office. I knocked on his door. "Come in," he said from inside.

"Hey, Reggie," Coach said enthusiastically. "Good to see you. Listen, I know what you're here for. I'm waiting too. I'm afraid I haven't heard anything yet. You'll be the first to know when I do, okay?"

The morning dragged on—history, then chemistry, then the dreaded third-period math class. Still, there was no word from Coach Clark regarding the suspension. When the noon bell rang, I knew it was time to head to the gym for the pep rally, but I still didn't know if I was going to be able to play.

The smile on Coach Clark's face provided the answer. As I entered the gym, he bounced up to me and shook my hand. "The district decided," he said. "No suspension. Nothing. They dismissed the whole case."

I was so relieved, I felt like turning cartwheels out on the basketball court along with the Lincoln cheerleaders. "What about the lawsuit?" I asked hopefully.

"Don't know yet," the coach said. "I guess we'll just have to see what Nate's parents decide to do. I would think, though, that they'd have the common sense to drop it."

I nodded. The situation wasn't completely resolved, but at least I'd get to play tonight. At least I wasn't going to be suspended for my senior season.

Midway through the pep rally, Coach Clark called the Lincoln co-captains—Lance Turner, Jeff Stevens and me—up to the microphone to say a few words.

When it was my turn, I grabbed the mike. "I'm just happy to be able to play tonight," I said. "I'm going to do my best to make you proud of this team. I'm sure the other guys will too."

The student section cheered. I felt a tingle run up and down my shoulders and arms. I wished the game could kick off right this second.

At about 5:00 PM, we all boarded two long yellow school buses for the ride to

Filmore. This was the usual drill for a road game. We put on all our gear in the Lincoln locker room and climbed on the bus, carrying our helmets. We were followed by a long line of parents' vehicles, booster club buses and cheerleading squad vans.

Filmore was a forty-five-minute ride away, through downtown to the northern outskirts of the city. It was the newest high-end suburb, full of lawyers and accountants and other professionals and their families. In contrast, our neighborhood was much more varied. We had kids like Jeff Stevens from rich families, kids from average families like mine and those from poorer neighborhoods too. Everybody was lumped together at Lincoln.

The bus trip gave me time to think about the last two weeks. It had been quite a rollercoaster ride: first Nate's injury, then finding out about Dad's anxiety, facing my own problems, the fiery encounters with Nate's mom, and finally wondering whether I'd be suspended. It would be nice tonight to forget about all that and just play football.

It was the perfect evening for a game— clear, crisp and with a slight chill in the air that signaled winter was just around the corner. Filmore played its games in a new stadium that must have seated nearly six thousand people. Even as we began warm-ups, it was close to being full.

The Filmore Friars weren't rated as highly as Lincoln, Milbury or Franklin. But we knew they were no pushovers, especially playing on their home field. Coach Clark gathered us on the sidelines, just before the opening kickoff. "Concentrate on the moment, boys," he warned. "Don't think ahead, even one play. We've got to get this one."

Coach must have sensed something about this game. Right from the start, it seemed that for some reason we weren't sharp, especially on the offensive side of the ball. Lance Turner didn't have his usual accuracy throwing the football. When he did toss a good pass, reliable receivers like Jeff Stevens weren't catching it.

The saving grace for Lincoln was that our defense was bottling up Filmore's attack. They couldn't get anything going, either. And Dr. MacIntyre's centering technique was working brilliantly for me. By halftime, I had six solo tackles in a scoreless tie.

As the game clock dwindled down to the last five minutes, our teams were tied 3–3. We had been lucky to get the three points we had. Our offense had barely moved the chains all night. The only way we'd managed to score was when I recovered a fumble at the Filmore thirty and Kyle Nance nailed an impressive forty-yard field goal. Filmore's points had come after its best offensive drive of the evening stalled out on our thirty. The Friars settled for three as well.

Now, with nobody playing well offensively, the game had boiled down to five minutes. Whichever defense held up better would decide the outcome.

Filmore had the ball at its own thirty to begin the series. I expected the Friars to stay conservative and keep the ball along the ground. Filmore's passing game had been sloppy. I was sure that their coaching staff wasn't going to risk a game-deciding interception at this late stage. Even a tie against Lincoln would be seen as a huge upset for the Friars. They didn't want to blow this opportunity.

On second down, Filmore quarterback Steve Akins dropped back and looked downfield for a receiver. For a second or two, I hung back, just in case he really did intend to pass. But then I bolted forward aggressively. I was certain they weren't throwing the ball. Not in this situation.

I burst into the backfield. By this time, Akins was rolling right, his halfback slightly behind him and to the outside. I shot between them, just in time to step in front of the pitchout that Akins had flipped toward his teammate. I saw the ball hanging in midair. I reached out my right hand and tapped it up. Then I grabbed it with my left.

There was nobody ahead of me upfield, so I turned on the jets. I took a quick look behind and saw Akins closing on me. The kid had some speed. I began to angle the other way, trying to use the width of the field to my advantage. But Akins was closing the gap between us, eating up turf with each stride. I sensed the Filmore quarterback leaping for me. I felt his arm brush my leg, and I high-stepped to avoid his grasp. He crashed to the turf, clutching only air. I sped into the end zone untouched. The Filmore crowd sat in stunned silence.

I turned around and headed upfield, only to be mobbed by a sea of white Lincoln jerseys. My teammates were pushing and shoving and grabbing my arms, shoulders and helmet. "Take it easy!" Coach Molloy yelled. "Leave the kid in one piece."

Kyle Nance booted the extra point, giving us a 10-3 lead. There were three minutes left, and Filmore had one series to get even. It wasn't over yet.

Kyle didn't get his toe completely into the kickoff, which resulted in Filmore getting a good return to its own forty. From there, Steve Akins, anxious to make amends for my turnover and touchdown, efficiently marshaled his offense to our thirty. As instructed by Coach Molloy, we were in a "prevent" defense. We weren't willing to give up anything long so, consequently, Akins had picked us apart with short passes.

But the Filmore quarterback was also running out of time. There were just thirty seconds left on the clock as he lined up for a first down on our thirty. The Friars had time for maybe three more plays, tops.

On first down, I batted away a pass intended for Filmore's tight end. On second, Akins missed a receiver streaking on a side-line pattern. Filmore called a time-out, with eight seconds left in the game, needing thirty yards for a score. One stop was all we needed to hold on to this win.

Steve Akins again lined up to take the snap. Before the ball was released, however, he stepped back three yards. They were using the shotgun, just like Franklin had done in the late-going against us. The ball was snapped cleanly to Akins, who began to roll to his left. I drew a bead on where he was headed and burst through an opening in the Filmore line.

I was closing in on Akins. I could see his eyes widen as he fought desperately to get to the outside so he could avoid my tackle. I launched myself at him, but something stopped me in mid-flight. Milt Davis, the squat, muscular fullback for Filmore, had laid on a perfect block. It flattened me cleanly before I could reach his quarterback.

Steve Akins instinctively followed the superb block of his teammate, heading quickly up field. From where I lay on the turf, I could see that only Bryce Clark stood between the Filmore quarterback and the end zone. Bryce moved in on Akins, lowered his shoulder and ploughed into the Filmore star's chest. The blow knocked Akins off-stride just long enough for three of our teammates to catch up and finish off the tackle. The game was over. We had won.

The entire Lincoln offensive team burst off the sidelines and onto the field. They mobbed a smiling Bryce, who this time had come up with the key play just when we needed it most.

Inside the locker room, Coach Clark walked over to my stall. "Boys, the game ball goes to our defensive leader and middle linebacker, Reggie," the coach said. "Heckuva game, son."

I stood up with the ball in my hand. "Thanks, Coach, but I think somebody else in here deserves this more."

I turned and flipped the football under-hand to Bryce Clark. He had earned it just as much, or more, than me. But it would have been tough for Coach to give it to his own son. Not tough for me, though.

Just like the geese, we all took turns leading on this team.

Bryce beamed my way. "Good to have you back, Stick-'em," he smiled.

It was good to be back. Nickname and all.

chapter fifteen

The next month flew by in a blur of football, school and homework. Our Lincoln varsity team romped to easy wins over district lightweights Milton, Peabody, Kline and Jefferson. We now had a record of five wins, zero losses and one tie with only a single game left on the schedule—the makeup contest against the Milbury Miners.

The season was coming to a close in dramatic fashion. Although the Franklin Demons had fallen off the pace with upset losses to Jefferson and Kline, they had managed to play Milbury to a draw as well. That left the Miners and our team dead-locked, each with 5-0-1 records. The final game of the season would determine the district championship and which team advanced to the regional playoffs.

Everybody at school was keyed up. Unfortunately for us, this was now a road game. Even though we were supposed to have played Milbury at home, the makeup contest was rescheduled for their stadium because ours had been booked for a junior college playoff. Playing on the road would make things tougher on us. But I was confident we could handle Milbury and its home crowd.

Coach Clark was intense all that week, using the third-stringers to run the Milbury offense so that our defense could get a feel for playing against it. The Miners used a formation that resembled something a pro team might run, mainly because Keith

Hobart had emerged as the best passing prep quarterback the city had ever seen.

I could tell Coach Clark was nervous about defending against the Miners' offense. He was a little more edgy than usual during practice. On Tuesday night, when I failed to pick up third-string fullback Terry Roberts coming out of the backfield for a swing pass, he let me have it. "C'mon, Scott, we absolutely need to get on that quicker!"

My ears burned at the criticism, but I understood Coach Clark's intensity. Our school hadn't advanced to the regionals in ten years. Coach was itching to end that streak. We all were.

As the week went on, I woke up progressively earlier each morning. I was so pumped for the Milbury game that I could barely concentrate on school. It seemed like Friday would never come.

On Friday morning, my clock radio read 5:45 AM as I headed downstairs. I heard the paper land with a thud on the step as

I approached the front door. It wasn't often that I beat the paperboy to the punch.

I opened the door and picked up the *Times*. I knew there would be an article setting up our game tonight. It was the biggest prep football matchup of the season. Everybody in the city would be keeping an eye on Miner Stadium.

Milbury hosts prep grudge match, the headline read. Underneath, a smaller secondary headline declared: *Miners seek revenge tonight for fallen teammate.*

My heart sank. Instead of previewing the great collision between the league's top two teams, it looked like the *Times* was trying to dredge up what had happened to Nate Brown. What was the point of that?

I read the story below. It didn't really back up the headlines. Milbury coach Phil Carter had said, *"We miss Nate in our lineup, and we're looking forward to seeing Lincoln again."* That was it. Nobody had said anything about there being a grudge between the teams. None of the players or coaches quoted had mentioned the word "revenge."

I showed Dad the newspaper. "What's with these guys?" he said, shaking his head. "Nate's injury has nothing to do with this game. It's a pretty cheap way to sell papers."

I had to agree. No matter what, I wasn't going to let this bother me. Not now. Tonight's game was too important.

At noon, Lincoln hosted the biggest pep rally I had ever seen. Former Lincoln varsity football players were there, so were city councilors and school board trustees. Channel 5 sportscaster Rick Santiago showed up with his camerawoman to interview Coach Clark and Lance Turner. That's when I knew that we had officially hit the big time.

Once again, we dressed at Lincoln and boarded the school bus for the ride to Milbury. This was only going to be a short trip. Milbury was just three miles away, on the eastern edge of the city. We were neighboring schools. The Miners and the Lions had always been huge football rivals, no matter how our respective seasons were going. The fact that we were both undefeated and on a collision course for the district title made the rivalry that much more exciting.

There was a traffic jam outside the parking lot at the Milbury stadium. Instead of waiting until the driver could pull in, Coach Clark told us to grab our helmets and get off the bus. As we walked through the parking lot, there were hundreds of Milbury fans, milling about portable barbecues and lazing on lawn chairs, enjoying a massive tailgate party. I'd never seen an atmosphere quite like this for a high school game.

The stands were packed, and the stadium lights were on by the time the officiating crew called our three co-captains to midfield for the coin toss. We won, electing to receive the ball first. Milbury chose to defend the south goal.

Just before the kickoff, the Milbury announcer said, "Ladies and gentlemen, boys and girls. Welcome to Miner Stadium, home of your Milbury Miners."

The crowd erupted. The cheerleaders waved their pom-poms. The giant Miner mascot swung his pickaxe menacingly toward our side of the field. Our over-stuffed Lion roared back at him through his megaphone.

"Before we begin tonight's game, I'd like to have your attention for a special introduction," the announcer continued. The crowd hushed. "Please welcome back to Miner Stadium to take the ceremonial kickoff, Milbury's own Nate Brown!"

The crowd went wild. Everybody in the stadium, including the close to two thousand Lincoln fans dressed in black and white, stood and applauded. Nate Brown came from the Milbury sideline, walking with the aid of a cane. I couldn't believe how quickly he made it out to midfield.

Nate waved at the crowd on both sides of the grandstand. Then he hobbled up to the football and gingerly tapped it off the tee a few yards with his right foot. Again, the fans roared. For a kid who had recently been lying in a hospital bed wondering if he'd ever walk again, he'd come a long way.

The Milbury co-captains shook Nate's hand and tousled his hair. I knew what I had to do. I broke ranks with my co-captains and trotted toward Nate. He extended his hand, and I grabbed it, pulling him toward me for a bear hug. Again the crowd cheered. "It's great to see you here, man," I said into his ear.

Nate grinned at me. "Thanks," he said. "The only thing better would be playing. But the district is letting me save my senior season for next fall. They're giving me an extra year of eligibility."

"That's awesome," I said. "Good luck tonight...but not too much luck."

Nate smiled again. "We don't need luck here at Milbury," he said with a wink.

The contest that followed lived up to the excitement created by the pre-game drama. Both teams wanted desperately to win, and both of us played like it. Heading into the fourth quarter, it was tied 21–21. The game had already featured plenty of hard-hitting defense and awesome offense.

Each team had a couple of promising fourth-quarter drives end prematurely. Milbury's faltered when Bryce Clark intercepted a Keith Hobart pass at our thirty yard line, snuffing out a great scoring chance for the Miners. Just a few minutes later, a Lincoln drive was stopped when Lance Turner fumbled at the Miners' forty.

The teams then exchanged fruitless possessions that ended in fourth-down punts. With two minutes left in the fourth quarter, Milbury had the ball at its own ten yard line. The Miners' bench called a time-out.

Coach Clark huddled us all together, the defense immediately around him and the offense circling us. "Boys, this has been a heckuva game," he said. "We're going to see if we can stop these guys one more time. If we're lucky, we'll get the ball back and pull this thing out. But first we've got to stop them."

Coach Molloy went over the defense. He was putting us in the "prevent" once again. I knew we'd be susceptible to short passes and runs, but at least we wouldn't give up anything long. It was a smart strategy. As I took the field with my teammates, I just hoped it worked.

Milbury was clearly expecting our tactic. Keith Hobart expertly squeezed a handful of first downs out of our defense. He passed to his speedy receivers on short routes, just inside our defensive coverage, and handed off to his backs. He was mixing things up like a master, probing our defense just enough to get the first downs his team needed.

With thirty seconds left, Milbury had the ball at our thirty yard line. Coach Clark called our final time-out. He looked across the field as he addressed us for the last time. "They're sending out their field-goal unit," he said. "Let's go for the block. We can't afford to let them make this kick. It's our only choice."

The coach set up a play that called for our line to open up a hole directly to the left of their center. I was to blitz hard through that hole and jump as high as I could. The timing had to be just right if I wanted to get a piece of the football.

Sure enough, Milbury went into their field-goal formation. Keith Hobart barked out the signals. Milbury's center snapped the ball crisply to Hobart, who brought it toward the turf to set up for Jerry Ryan's place-kick.

I watched all of this play out as I jetted through the hole our defense had opened up on the Milbury line. I planned to be nearing Hobart just as Ryan stepped into his kick. That would give me the best chance to block it.

It happened in a millisecond, before I could comprehend what was going on. As Keith Hobart began to pull the football toward the turf, he suddenly stopped, popped up, pivoted and took off at full speed to his left. It was a fake field goal.

By this time, I had already committed to going for the block. All I could do was watch helplessly as Hobart turned the corner and headed for the end zone. Everybody else on our defense had been fooled too. The smooth Milbury quarterback waltzed across the goal line untouched. The Miners had won. The crowd went crazy.

I pulled myself up from the turf slowly, looking over to the Milbury sidelines. The Miners had already dumped a barrel of Gatorade over the head of Phil Carter, their head coach. The Miners were jumping up and down, their hands stretched toward the sky. In the middle of the pack, doing his best to summon up a jump was Nate Brown.

I felt badly for my teammates and for Coach Clark. But something about seeing Nate on his feet and celebrating a football victory almost made up for the deep disappointment I felt.

I put my arm around Bryce Clark, who had played his heart out. He was crying, now that we had fallen just short. "You'll be back here next year," I said to him. "And you'll win that one."

Everybody on our team had already headed into the locker room for the postgame talk. I was about to join them, when I heard my name being called from the near-empty Lincoln sidelines. I spun around. It was Dr. MacIntyre. With him was a tall man in a gray suit carrying a black notebook.

"Hey, Reggie, great game," Dr. MacIntyre said, approaching me. "Look, I know you're busy but I just want you to meet someone really quick."

"Sure," I said, stepping toward the man in the gray suit, my sweaty hand outstretched.

"This is Milt Black," Dr. MacIntyre said. "He's from the Tech football program."

Instantly, I was nervous. I'd never talked to a college recruiter before. Come to think of it, I'd never even seen one.

"Dr. Mac has told me a lot about you, Reggie," the man said. "I just wanted to meet you and let you know that we've been watching you a lot this season. If you're interested, we'd like to talk to you seriously about playing some more football after high school."

My head was spinning. I was still bitterly disappointed by the loss, but at the same time totally exhilarated about having a Tech football scout actually interested in me.

"Sure." I grinned. "I'd love that."

"I'll give you a call this week," Mr. Black said. "Now, you'd better scoot into the locker room. I know Coach Clark likes everybody in there as soon as possible."

I thanked both men and jogged quickly to join my teammates. The room smelled like a mixture of tears and sweat. The mood was about what you'd expect from a bunch of kids who had worked their butts off only to fall one play short.

Coach Clark kept his wrap-up talk to five minutes. It was all positive. This wasn't a time to criticize or to dwell on what might have been, he said, but to celebrate. "I'm proud of each one of you boys," he concluded. I felt bad for Coach. He had come so close to making his first trip to regionals as a head coach.

We all slowly changed into our street clothes for the ride back to Lincoln. It remained pretty quiet in the locker room. Everybody was digesting the loss, most of all the seniors like me. We had played our last game in a Lincoln uniform. Maybe it was easier for me than some kids. At least

I'd probably be playing football somewhere next year.

"Reggie," Jeff Stevens called from his spot near the locker room door. "Somebody here to see you."

That was weird. In four years of football at Lincoln, I don't think anybody had ever knocked on the locker room door to pull me out.

I pulled on a clean T-shirt and walked outside, still wearing my dirty football pants and cleats. On the other side of the door stood Nate's mother.

She stepped forward and offered me her hand. I shook it, not knowing what was coming next. A few seconds of awkward silence followed. "Reggie," she finally said, "I just wanted to tell you that I'm sorry. When Nate got hurt, I was just so angry. I was looking for somebody to blame. I took it out on you. I..."

I could tell that she was on the verge of tears. "It's good to see you out on the field again," she said.

"Thanks." I wasn't sure what else to say.

She turned to walk away. "Mrs. Brown," I called after her, "I hope Nate's back out here soon too."

She managed a weak smile. "It might be awhile before he's ready," she said. "And before I'm ready too."

I nodded. The last couple of months hadn't been easy. But as I turned back toward the locker room, I was pretty sure the worst of it was over.